The **SPILLANE** of
I, The Jury and
Kiss Me, Deadly fame
does it again with
THE SNAKE.

Made to order for the no-holds-barred Spillane fans,
this is a yarn of violence and vengeance that zeroes
Mike Hammer into the middle of an old, old crime.

Velda—Hammer's voluptuous, long-lost love takes in
a baby-faced blonde, a kiss-me-deadly type who's running
away from a rich stepfather she hates and fears.
When two gunmen come shooting for the runaway,
Hammer takes over.

Crooked politicos, snarling hoods and sex-hungry females
all try to slow down the two-fisted private eye, but
Hammer smashes it out to the desperate end . . . to a
grisly and shocking solution that tops anything Spillane
has ever written, anything that you have ever read.

SIGNET Thrillers by Mickey Spillane

(0451)

- [ ] **THE BIG KILL** (134346—$2.95)*
- [ ] **BLOODY SUNRISE** (120507—$2.25)
- [ ] **THE BODY LOVERS** (127951—$2.50)*
- [ ] **THE BY-PASS CONTROL** (092260—$1.75)
- [ ] **THE DAY OF THE GUNS** (129857—$2.50)*
- [ ] **THE DEATH DEALERS** (129849—$2.50)*
- [ ] **THE DEEP** (121031—$2.50)
- [ ] **THE DELTA FACTOR** (122089—$2.50)
- [ ] **THE ERECTION SET** (131452—$3.50)*
- [ ] **THE GIRL HUNTERS** (129830—$2.50)*
- [ ] **I, THE JURY** (113969—$2.95)
- [ ] **KILLER MINE** (117972—$1.50)
- [ ] **THE LAST COP OUT** (119053—$2.50)
- [ ] **THE LONG WAIT** (121902—$2.50)
- [ ] **ME, HOOD** (116798—$1.95)
- [ ] **MY GUN IS QUICK** (097912—$1.95)
- [ ] **ONE LONELY NIGHT** (121651—$2.50)
- [ ] **THE SNAKE** (122091—$2.50)
- [ ] **SURVIVAL ... ZERO** (121058—$2.50)
- [ ] **THE TOUGH GUYS** (092252—$1.75)
- [ ] **THE TWISTED THING** (122070—$2.50)
- [ ] **VENGEANCE IS MINE** (132645—$2.50)*

*Prices slightly higher in Canada

MICKEY SPILLANE

The
SNAKE

A SIGNET BOOK
NEW AMERICAN LIBRARY

For Bob Fellows, who knows Mike
from too many angles.
And Donna, who knows Bob the
same way.

PUBLISHER'S NOTE

COPYRIGHT, ©, 1964 BY MICKEY SPILLANE

Published by arrangement with E. P. Dutton and Company, Inc.

 SIGNET TRADEMARK REG. U.S. PAT. OFF. AND FOREIGN COUNTRIES
REGISTERED TRADEMARK—MARCA REGISTRADA
HECHO EN CHICAGO, U.S.A.

SIGNET, SIGNET CLASSIC, MENTOR, PLUME, MERIDIAN AND NAL
BOOKS *are published by New American Library,*
1633 Broadway, New York, New York 10019

FIRST SIGNET PRINTING, NOVEMBER, 1964

11 12 13 14 15 16 17 18 19

Printed in Canada

CHAPTER ONE

You walk down the street at night. It's raining out. The only sound is that of your own feet. There are city sounds too, but these you don't hear because at the end of the street is the woman you've been waiting for for seven long years and each muffled tread of your footsteps takes you closer and closer and the sound of them marks off seconds and days and months of waiting.

Then, suddenly, you're there, outside a dark-faced building, a brownstone anachronism that stares back dully with the defiant expression of the moronic and you have an impending sense of being challenged.

What would it be like, I thought. *Was she still beautiful? Had seven years of hell changed her as it had me? And what did you say to a woman you loved and thought was killed because you pulled a stupid play? How do you go from seven years ago to now?*

Only a little while ago a lot of other feet were pointing this way, searching for this one house on this one street, but now mine were the only ones left to find it because the rest belonged to dead men or those about to die.

The woman inside was important now. Perhaps the most important in the world. What she knew would help destroy an enemy when she told it. My hands in my pockets balled into hard knots to keep from shaking and for a moment the throbbing ache of the welts and cuts that laced my skin stopped.

And I took the first step.

There were five more, then the V code on the doorbell marked *Case*, the automatic clicking of the lock and I was in the vestibule of the building under a dim yellow light from a single overhead bulb and down the shadowed hallway to the rear was the big door. Behind it lay seven years ago.

I tapped out a Y on the panel and waited, then tapped a slow R and the bolt slid back and the knob turned

5

and there she stood with the gun still ready if something had gone wrong.

Even in that pale light I could see that she was more beautiful than ever, the black shadow of her hair framing a face I had seen every night in the misery of sleep for so long. Those deep brown eyes still had that hungry look when they watched mine and the lush fullness of her mouth glistened with a damp warmth of invitation.

Then, as though there had never been those seven years, I said, "Hello, Velda."

For a long second she just stood there, somehow telling me that it was only the *now* that counted and with that same rich voice that could make music with a simple word, she answered, "Mike . . ."

She came into my arms with a rush and buried her face in my neck, barely able to whisper my name over and over because my arms were so tight around her. Even though I knew I was hurting her I couldn't stop and she didn't ask me to. It was like we were trying to get inside each other and in the frenzy of it found a way when our mouths met in a predatory coupling we had never known before. I tasted the fire and beauty of her, my fingers probing the flesh of her back and arms and shoulders, leaving marks wherever they touched. That familiar resiliency was still in her body, tightening gradually into a passionate tautness that rippled and quivered, crying out soundlessly for more, more, more.

I took the gun from her hand, dropped it in a chair, then pushed the door closed with my foot and felt for the light switch. A lamp on the table seemed to come alive with the unreal slowness of a movie prop, gradually highlighting the classic beauty of her face and the provocative thrust of her breasts.

There was a subtle leanness about her now, like you saw in those fresh from a battle area, every gesture a precision movement, every sense totally alert. And now she was just beginning to realize that it was over and she could be free again.

"Hello, kitten," I said, and watched her smile.

There wasn't much we could say. That would take time, but now we had all the time in the world. She looked at me, talking through those crazy eyes, then her expression went soft and a frown made small creases

6

across her forehead. Her fingers went out and touched my face and the white edge of her teeth went into her lip.

"Mike . . . ?"

"It's okay, baby."

"You're not . . . hurt?"

I shook my head. "Not any more."

"There's something about you now . . . I can't quite tell what. . . ."

"Seven years, Velda," I interrupted. "It was downhill all the way until I found out you were still alive. It leaves marks, but none that can't be wiped out."

Her eyes blurred under tears that came too quickly to control. "Mike darling, . . . I couldn't reach you. It was all too impossible and big . . ."

"I know it, kid. You don't have to explain."

Her hair swirled in a dark arc when she shook her head. "But I do."

"Later."

"Now." Her fingers touched my mouth to silence me and I let them. "It took seven years to learn a man's secret and escape Communist Europe with information that will keep us equal or better than they are. I know I could have . . . gotten away earlier . . . but I had to make a choice."

"You made the right one."

"There was no way to tell you."

"I know it."

"Truly . . ."

"I understand, kitten."

She wouldn't listen. Her voice was softly insistent, almost pleading. "I could have, Mike. I know I could have some way, but I couldn't afford the chance. There were millions of lives at stake." She paused a second, then pulled my cheek against hers. "I know how you must have felt, thinking you had me killed. I thought of it so often I nearly went out of my mind, but I still couldn't have changed things."

"Forget it," I told her.

"What did happen to you, Mike?"

She pushed away, holding me at arm's length to study me.

"I got to be a drunk," I said.

7

"You?"

"Me, kitten."

Her expression was one of curious bewilderment. "But when I told them . . . they had to find you . . . only you could do it . . ."

"One mentioned your name and I changed, honey. When you came alive again, so did I."

"Oh, Mike . . ."

As big as she was, I picked her up easily, kissed her again, and took her across the room to the gaudy mohair couch that nestled in the bay of an airshaft window. She quivered against me, smiled when I laid her down, then pulled my mouth to hers with a desperation that told me of the loneliness of seven years and the gnawing wanting inside her now.

Finally she said, "I'm a virgin, Mike."

"I know."

"I've always waited for you. It's been a pretty long wait."

I grinned down at her. "I was crazy to make you wait."

"And now?"

Then I wasn't grinning any more. She was all mine whenever I wanted her, a big, beautiful animal of a woman who loved me and was ready to be taken *now, now*. Even touching was a painful emotion and the fire that had been dormant was one I didn't want to put out.

I said, "Can you wait a little bit more?"

"Mike?" There was a quick hurt in her eyes, then the question.

"Let's do it right, kitten. Always I do the wrong things. Let's make this one right." Before she could answer I said, "Don't argue. Don't even talk about it. We do it, that's all, then we can explode into a million pieces. We do the bit at City Hall with the license and do it right."

Velda smiled back impishly, the happiness of knowing what I wanted plain in her face. "That really doesn't matter," she told me. "First I want you. Now. More than ever."

"Crazy broad," I said, then fought her mouth with mine, knowing we were both going to win. My hand drifted across the satiny expanse of her naked shoulder, feeling the minute trembling throughout her body. She twisted so she pressed against me, moaning softly, demanding things we never had from each other.

Pretty," he said from the door. *"Real pretty."*

I still had the .45 in my belt but I never could have made it. Velda's convulsive grip around my neck slowed the action enough so that I saw the Police Positive in his hand and didn't get killed after all. The hammer was back for faster shooting and the look on his face was one I had seen before on other cheap killers and knew that he'd drop me the second he thought I might be trouble.

"Go on, don't stop," he said. "I like good shows."

I made my grin as simpering as I could, rolling away from Velda until I sat perched on the edge of the couch. I was going wild inside and fought to keep my hands dangling at my sides while I tried to look like an idiot caught in the act until I could think my way past this thing.

"I didn't know there'd be two but it figures a babe like you'd have something going for her." He nudged the gun toward me. "But why grab off a mutt like this, baby?"

When she spoke from behind me her voice was completely changed. "When I could have had you?"

"That's the way, baby. I've been watching you through that window four days and right now I'm ready. How about that?"

I would have gone for the rod right then, but I felt the pressure of her knee against my back.

"How about that?" Velda repeated.

The guy let out a jerky laugh and looked at me through slitted eyes. "So maybe we'll make music after all, kid. Just as soon as I dump the mutt here."

Then I couldn't keep quiet any longer. "You're going to have to do it the hard way."

The gun shifted just enough so it pointed straight at my head. "That's the way I always do things, mutt."

He was ready. The gun was tight in his hand and the look was there and he was ready. Velda said, "Once that gun goes off you won't have me."

It wasn't enough. The guy laughed again and nodded. "That's okay too, baby. This is what I came for anyway."

9

"Why?" she asked him.

"Games, baby?" The gun swung gently toward her, then back to me, ready to take either or both of us when he wanted to. I tried to let fear bust through the hate inside me and hoped it showed like that when I slumped a little on the couch. My hand was an inch nearer the .45 now, but still too far away.

"I want the kid, baby, ya know?" he said. "So no games. Trot her out, I take off, and you stay alive."

"Maybe," I said.

His eyes roved over me. "Yeah, maybe," he grinned. "You know something, mutt? You ain't scared enough. You're thinking."

"Why not?"

"Sure, why not? But whatever you think it just ain't there for you, mutt. This ain't your day."

There were only seconds now. He was past being ready and his eyes said it was as good as done and I was dead and he started that final squeeze as Velda and I moved together.

We never would have made it if the door hadn't slammed open into him and knocked his arm up. The shot went into the ceiling and with a startled yell he spun around toward the two guys in the doorway, dropping as he fired, but the smaller guy got him first with two quick shots in the chest and he started to tumble backwards with the blood bubbling in his throat.

I was tangled in the raincoat trying to get at my gun when the bigger one saw me, streaked off a shot that went by my head, and in the light of the blast I knew they weren't cops because I recognized a face of a hood I knew a long time. It was the last shot he ever made. I caught him head on with a .45 that pitched him back through the door. The other one tried to nail me while I was rolling away from Velda and forgot about the guy dying on the floor. The mug let one go from the Police Positive that ripped into the hood's belly and with a choking yell he tumbled out the door, tripped, and hobbled off out of sight, calling to someone that he'd been hit.

I kicked the gun out of the hand of the guy on the floor, stepped over him, and went out in the hall gun first. It was too late. The car was pulling away from the curb and all that was left was the peculiar silence of the street.

He was on his way out when I got back to him, the sag of death in his face. There were things I wanted to ask him, but I never got the chance. Through bloody froth he said, "You'll . . . get yours, mutt."

I didn't want him to die happy. I said, "No chance, punk. This is my day after all."

His mouth opened in a grimace of hate and frustration that was the last living thing he ever did.

From where to where, I thought. *Why are there always dead men around me? I came back, all right. Just like in the old days. Love and death going hand in hand.*

There was something familiar about his face. I turned his head with my toe, looked at him closely and caught it. Velda said, "Do you know him?"

"Yeah. His name is Basil Levitt. He used to be a private dick until he tried a shakedown on somebody who wouldn't take it, then he did time for second-degree murder."

"What about the other one?"

"They call him Kid Hand. He was a free-lance gun that did muscle for small bookies on bettors who didn't want to pay off. He's had a fall before too."

I looked at Velda and saw the way she was breathing and the set expression on her face. There was a strange sort of wildness there you find on animals suddenly having to fight for their lives. I said, "They aren't from the other side, kitten. These are new ones. These want something different." I waited a moment, then: "Who's the kid, honey?"

"Mike . . ."

I pointed to the one on the floor. "He came for a kid. He came here ready to shoot you up. Now who's the kid?"

Again, she gave me an anguished glance. "A girl . . . she's only a young girl."

I snapped my fingers impatiently. "Come on, give me, damn it. You know where you stand! How many people have died because of what you know and right now you haven't got rid of it. You want to get killed after everything that happened for some stupid reason?"

"All right, Mike." Anguish gave way to concern then

and she glanced upward. "Right now she's in an empty room on the top floor. Directly over this one."

"Okay, who is she?"

"I . . . don't know. She came here the day after . . . I was brought here. I heard her crying outside and took her in."

"That wasn't very smart."

"Mike . . . there were times when I wish someone had done that to me."

"Sorry."

"She was young, desperate, in trouble. I took care of her. It was like taking in a scared rabbit. Whatever her trouble was, it was big enough. I thought I'd give her time to quiet down, then perhaps be able to help her."

"What happened?"

"She's scared, Mike. Terrified. She's all mixed up and I'm the only one she can hang on to."

"Good, I'll take your word for it. Now get me up to her before this place is crawling with cops. We have about five minutes before somebody is going to be curious enough to make a phone call."

From the third floor you could hear the rhythmic tap of her feet dancing a staccato number that made you think of an Eleanor Powell routine when prettylegs was queen of the boards. There was no music, yet you knew *she* heard some and was in a never-never land of her own.

Velda knocked but the dancing didn't stop. She turned the knob and pushed the door open and with a soft cry the girl in the middle of the room twisted around, her hand going to her mouth when she saw me, huge eyes darting from Velda's to mine. She threw one glance toward the window when Velda said, "It's all right, Sue. This is our friend."

It was going to take more than that to convince her and there wasn't enough time. "My name is Mike Hammer, Sue. I'm going to help you. Can you understand that?"

Whatever it was, it worked. The fear left her face and she tried on a tentative smile and nodded. "Will you . . . really?"

12

"Really," I nodded back. To Velda I said, "Can we get her out of here?"

"Yes. I know of a place I can take her."

"Where?"

"Do you remember Connie Lewis' restaurant on Forty-first?"

"Just off Ninth?"

"That's it. I'll be there. She has the upper three floors to herself."

"That was seven years ago."

"She'll be there," Velda told me.

"Okay," I said, "you get there with the kid. I'll do the talking on the bit downstairs, then in about an hour you show up at Pat's office. I'm being a damn fool for letting you out on the street again but I can't see any other way of doing it."

Her hand squeezed mine and she smiled. "It'll be all right, Mike."

Then the kid walked up and I looked into the face of the prettiest little Lolita-type I ever saw. She was a tiny blonde with enormous brown eyes and a lovely mouth in a pert pointed face that made you want to pick her up like a doll. Her hair was silk-soft and hung loosely to her shoulders and when she moved all you could see was girl-woman and if you weren't careful you'd feel the wrong kind of feel.

But I was an old soldier who had been there and back, so I said, "How old are you, chicken?"

She smiled and said, "Twenty-one."

I grinned at Velda. "She's not lying. You thought she was kidding when she told you that, didn't you?"

Velda nodded.

"We'll get straight on this later. Right now take off." I looked at Sue, reaching out to feel her hair. "I don't know what your trouble is, girl, but first things first. I'm going to lay something on the line with you though."

"Oh?"

"Downstairs there are two dead men because of you. So play it the way you're told and we'll make it. Try using your own little head and there may be more dead people. Me, I've had it. I'll help you all the way

13

as long as you do it like I say, but go on your own and you're like out, kid, understand? There aren't any more people who can make this boy tumble again, big or little. I'm telling you this because you're not as little as you look. You can fool a lot of slobs, but not this slob, so we're starting off square, okay?"

"Okay, Mr. Hammer." There was no hesitation at all.

"Call me Mike."

"Sure, Mike."

"Get her out of here, Velda."

The sirens converged from both directions. They locked the street in on either end and two more took the street to the front of the house. The floods hit the doorway and the uniformed cops came in with .38's in their hands.

I had the door open, the lights lit, and both hands in view when the first pair stepped through the doorway. Before they asked I took the position, let them see my .45 on the table beside the other guns, and watched patiently while they flipped open my wallet with the very special ticket in the identification window.

The reaction was slow at first. They weren't about to take any chances with two dead men on the floor, but they couldn't go too far the other way either. Finally the older one handed my wallet back. "I knew you back in the old days, Mike."

"Times haven't changed much."

"I wonder." He nodded toward the two bodies. "I don't suppose you want to explain about all this now?"

"That's right."

"You got a big ticket there. When?"

"Call Captain Chambers. This is his baby."

"I guess it is."

"There's a new Inspector in the division. He might not like the action."

"No sweat, friend. Don't worry."

"I'm not worrying. I just remember you and Captain Chambers were friends."

"No more."

"I heard that too." He holstered his gun. Behind him another pair came in cautiously, ready. "This a big one?" he asked.

14

"Yeah. Can I make a call?"

"Mind if I make it for you?"

"Nope." I gave him a number that he already knew and watched his face go flat when I handed him the name. He went outside to the car, put the call through, and when he came back there was a subtle touch of deference in his attitude. Whatever he had said to the others took the bull off me and by the time the M.E. got there it was like someone had diplomatic immunity.

Pat came in five minutes later. He waited until the pictures were taken and the bodies removed, then waved everybody else out except the little man in gray whom nobody was big enough to wave out. Then he studiously examined my big fat .45 and said, "The same one, isn't it?"

"It's the only one I ever needed."

"How many men have you killed with it?"

"Nine," I said. Then added, "With that gun."

"Good score."

"I'm still alive."

"Sometimes I wonder."

I grinned at him. "You hate me, buddy, but you're glad, aren't you?"

"That you're still alive?"

"Uh-huh."

He turned slowly, his eyes searching for some obscure answer. "I don't know," he said. "Sometimes I can't tell who is the worse off. Right now I'm not sure. It's hard to kill friendships. I tried hard enough with you and I almost made it work. Even with a woman between us I can't be sure any more. You crazy bastard, I watch what you do, see you get shot and beat to hell and wonder why it has to happen like that, and I'm afraid to tell myself the answer. I know it but I can't say it."

"So say it."

"Later."

"Okay."

"Now what happened?" He looked at Art Rickerby sitting in the chair.

I said, "Velda was here. I came for her. These two guys bust in, this one here first. The other came in time to break up the play."

15

"Nicely parlayed."

"Well put, buddy."

"For an ex-drunk you're doing all right." He glanced at Rickerby again.

"Some people have foresight," I reminded him.

"Do I leave now?" Pat said. "Do I go along with the Federal bit and take off?"

For the first time Art Rickerby spoke. He was quiet as always and I knew that there were no ends left untied in the past I had just left. He said, "Captain . . . there are times when . . . there are times. It was you who forced Mr. Hammer into circumstances he could hardly cope with. It was a dead man and me who made him stick to it. If he's anathema out of the past, then it's our fault. We brought a man back who should have died a long time ago. The present can't stand a man like that any more. Now they want indecision and compromise and reluctance and fear . . . and we've dropped a hot iron in society's lap. We've brought a man back who almost shouldn't be here and now you and me and society are stuck with him."

"Thanks a bunch," I said.

"Sure," Pat said to Art, "he's always been in the special-privilege class, but now it's over my head. You got the pull, Rickerby. I don't get all the picture, but I've been around long enough to figure a few things out. Just clue me on this one."

"Pat . . ." I started.

"Not you, Mike. *Him.*" He smiled with that gentle deceptiveness. "And make it good. We have two dead men here and I'm not writing that off for anybody. No more I'm not."

Art nodded and glanced at his watch. "The girl Velda," he said, "she was the crux. She has information this country depends upon. A team of assassins was assigned to kill her and nobody could get to that team we called 'The Dragon' but him because nobody could be as terrible as they were. It turned out that he was even worse. If that is a good word. For that information this country would pay any price and part of the cost was to rehabilitate this man in a sense and give him back his privilege and his gun.

"The Dragon team is gone now. There is only the

16

girl Velda. There is still that price to pay and he can call the tune. You have no choice but to back him up. Is that clear?"

"No, but it's coming through," Pat said. "I know most of the story but I find it hard to believe."

I said, "Pat . . ."

"What?"

"Let's leave it, kid. We were both right. So she's still mine. If you want her then take her away, but you have to fight me for her and you haven't got a chance in the world of winning."

"Not as long as you're alive," he told me.

"Sure, Pat."

"And the law of averages is on my side."

"Why sure."

I didn't think he could do it, but he did. He grinned and stuck out his hand and instinctively I took it. "Okay, boy. It's like before now. We start fresh. Do I get the story or does he?"

"First him, buddy," I said, nodding toward Art, "then you. It's bigger than local and I'm not just a private cop any more."

"They told me about your ticket. Smart."

"You know me. Never travel small."

"That's right. Somebody's got to be the hero."

"Nuts. If I'm on a dead play, then I want odds that will pay off."

"They did."

"Damn right they did. I stuck it up and broke it off. Everybody wanted me dead and instead it turned all the way around. So I got the payoff. A big ticket and the rod back and nobody puts the bull on me until I flub it royally . . . and this, friend, I'm not about to do again."

"No?"

"Watch."

"My pleasure, big buddy." He grinned. Again. "Mind if I leave and you talk it out with Mister Government here?"

"No. But be at your office soon. She'll be there and so will I."

"Soon?"

"An hour."

"I'll be waiting, hero."

When he left Art Rickerby said, "She has to talk right away. Where is she?"

"I told you . . . in an hour . . . at Pat's office."

"There were dead men here."

"So . . ."

"Don't piddle with me, Mike."

"Don't piddle with me, Art."

"Who were they?"

"I damn well don't know, but this you'll do and damn well do it right."

"Don't tell me what to do."

"No? I shove it up your tail if I want to, Art, and don't you forget it. You do this one my way. This is something else from your personal angle and leave it alone. Let those dead men be. As far as anybody is concerned they're part of The Dragon group and the last part at that. There ain't no more, the end, finis. They came for Velda and I was here to lay on the gravy like I did the rest and you go along with it. What's here is not part of your business at all, but for the moment you can cover me. Do it."

"Mike . . ."

"Just do it and shut up."

"Mike . . ."

I said softly, "I gave you The Dragon, didn't I?"

"Yes."

"I was dead. You exhumed me. You made me do things that were goddamned near impossible and when I didn't die doing them you were surprised. So be surprised now. Do like I tell you."

"Or . . . ?"

"Or Velda won't come in."

"You're sure?"

"Positive, friend."

"It will be done."

"Thanks."

"No trouble."

And Velda told them the next day. She spelled it out in detail and a government organization collapsed. In Moscow thirty men died and in the East Zone of Berlin five more disappeared and in South America

18

there was a series of accidents and several untimely deaths and across the face of the globe the living went to the dead in unaccountable numbers and codes and files were rearranged and meetings hastily brought about and summit conferences planned and in the U.N. buildings whole new philosophies were adopted and decisions brought about in a changed light and as suddenly as she had been a threat to a different world, she had become a person again. She had nothing more to give and in the world of politics there was no retribution as long as you knew nothing new and really didn't care at all.

But there *was* something new. There were two dead men to tell about it and somewhere in the city was another with a bullet in his gut looking for somebody to take it out and if the little blonde didn't tell, one of these would.

You just didn't lay dead men at your feet without someone coming looking for you.

And I had them at my feet.

CHAPTER TWO

I knew I had a tail on me when I left the D.A.'s office. It had been nicely set up even though Rickerby had put the fix in for me. No local police force likes to be queered out of a deal in their own back yard, and if they could move in, orders or not, they were going to give it the big try. If Pat had set the tail it would have been hard to spot, but the new D.A. was too ambitious to figure out there were civilian-type pros in the police business too.

For an hour I let him wait outside bars, fool around a department store while I picked up a few goodies, then went in one door of the Blue Ribbon Restaurant on Forty-fourth, around through the bar, and out that door while he was looking for me at the tables. I was back on Seventh Avenue before he knew I was gone, flagged down a cab, and had him cut over to Forty-ninth and Ninth.

Connie Lewis' place was called "La Sabre" and turned out to be a downstairs supper place for the neighborhood trade. It specialized in steaks and chops and seemed to be built around a huge charcoal grill that smoked and sizzled into a copper canopy. Connie was a round little woman with a perpetual smile and wrinkles at the corners of her eyes and mouth that said it was for real. It had been years since I had seen her and she hadn't changed a bit.

But me she didn't recognize at first. When it did come she beamed all over, tried to get me to drink, then eat, and when I wouldn't do either, showed me the way to the staircase going upstairs and told me Velda was on the second floor rear with her company.

I used the same VY knock and she opened the door. There was no gun in her hand this time, but I knew it wasn't far out of reach. She pulled me in, closed the door, and locked it. I grinned at her, grabbed her by the shoulders, and touched her mouth with mine. Lightly. I couldn't afford any more. Her eyes laughed back at me and told me I could pick my own time and place. Any time, any place.

I said, "Hello, beautiful. Where's the kid?"

"Here I am, Mike."

She eased into the room impishly, hands clasped behind her back. She stood at the corner of the bedroom door watching, seemingly unafraid, but inside those huge brown eyes was a worm of fear that had been there too long to be plucked out easily.

I took Velda's arm, steered her to the table, and motioned the kid to come over too. Automatically, the kid slid closer to Velda, knowing she was protected there, never taking her eyes from my face.

"Let's have it," I said.

Velda nodded. "You can tell him."

"I . . . don't know."

For what it was worth I took out my new wallet and flipped it open. The blue and gold card with the embossed seal in the plastic window did the trick again. She studied it, frowned, then made up her mind.

"All right," she finally told me. "My name is Sue Devon." When she said it there was a challenge in her voice I couldn't ignore.

"Am I supposed to know you?"

She flicked her eyes to her hands, to Velda, then to me. "I have another name."

"Oh?"

"Torrence. I never use it. He had me legally adopted a long time ago but I never use his name. I hate it."

I shook my head. "Sorry, kid. I don't make you at all."

Velda reached out and touched my hand. "Sim Torrence. He was the District Attorney once; now he's running in the primaries for governor of the state."

"Win with Sim?"

"That's right."

"I remember seeing posters around but I never tied him up with the D.A.'s office." I let a grin ease out. "It's been a rough seven years. I didn't keep up with politics. Now let's hear the rest of this."

Sue nodded, her hair tumbling around her face. She bit at her lip with even white teeth, her hands clasped

21

so tight the knuckles showed white. "I ran away from him."

"Why?"

The fear was a live thing in her eyes. "I think . . . he killed my mother. Now he wants to kill me."

When I glanced at Velda I knew she was thinking the same thing I was. I said, "People running for governor don't usually kill people."

"He killed my mother," she repeated.

"You said you *thought* he did." She didn't answer so I asked, "When was this supposed to have happened?"

"A long time ago."

"How long?"

"I . . . was a baby. Eighteen years ago."

"How do you know he did this?"

She wouldn't look at me. "I just know it, that's all."

"Honey," I said, "you can't accuse a man of murder with a reason like that."

She made a little shrug and worked her fingers together.

I said, "You have something else in your mind. What is it?"

Velda slipped her arm around her shoulders and squeezed. Sue looked at her gratefully and turned back to me again. "I remember Mama talking. Before she died. Whatever she said . . . is in my mind . . . but I can't pick out the words. I was terribly frightened. She was dying and she talked to me and told me something and I don't remember what it was!" She sucked her breath in and held it while the tears welled up in her eyes.

When she relaxed I said, "And what makes you think he wants to kill you?"

"I know . . . the way he looks at me. He . . . touches me."

"Better, baby. You'll have to do better than that."

"Very well. There was a car. It almost hit me."

"Did you recognize it?"

"No."

"Go on."

"There was a man one night. He followed me home from the theater. He tried to cut me off but I knew the roads and lost him not far from the house."

"Did you recognize him or his car?"

22

"No."

"Did you report the incidents?"

"No," she said softly.

"Okay, Sue, my turn. Do you know you're an exception-ally pretty girl?" She looked up at me. "Sure you do. Men are going to follow you, so get used to dodging. Nearly everybody has had a close call with a car, so don't put too much store in that. And so far as your stepfather is concerned, he'd look at you like any man would his daughter and touch you the same way. You haven't said anything concrete yet."

"Then what about that man you killed and the other one?"

"*Touché*," I said. But I couldn't let it lay there. She was waiting and she was scared. I looked at Velda. "Did you tell her where you've been for seven years and what happened?"

"She knows."

"And about me?"

"Everything."

"Then maybe this is an answer . . . those men were part of an enemy organization who had to destroy Velda before she talked. They moved in to get her, not you. And now it's over. Nobody's going to kill her because now she's said her piece and it's too late. What do you think about that?"

"I'm not going back," she said simply.

"Supposing I go see your stepfather. Suppose I can really find out the truth, even to what your mother told you. Would that help any?"

"Maybe." Her voice was a whisper.

"Okay, kid, I'll play Big Daddy."

Velda looked up with eyes so full of thanks I had to laugh at her. She scooted the kid off to the other end of the room, took my arm, and walked me to the door. "You'll do all you can?"

"You know, you'd think I'd know better by now."

"Mike . . . don't change."

"No chance, baby."

She opened the door. "Do you . . . believe that about . . . those men coming for me?"

After a few seconds I said, "No. Basil Levitt said he wanted both you and the kid so it wasn't anything

23

to do with the last operation. She's in it someplace."
I knew I was frowning.

"What are you thinking of?"

"Something he said, damn it." I wiped my face with
my hand and grimaced. "I've been away too long. I'm
not clicking."

"It will come."

"Sure, honey," I said. I touched her face lightly. "Later?"

"I'll be waiting."

"Put the kid to bed."

She made a face at me, grinned and nodded.

It was like there had never been those seven years
at all.

There wasn't much trouble getting background material
on Simpson Torrence. He had been making headlines
since the '30's, was featured in several of the latest magazines, and was the subject of three editorials in opposition
newspapers. I took two hours to go over the bits and
pieces and what I came up with made him a likely candidate
for governor. In fact, several of his high-ranking constituents were looking past the mansion at Albany to
the White House in Washington.

But good points I wasn't looking for. If there was
anything to the kid's story at all, then something would
have to point to another side of the guy's character.
People just don't come all good.

I called Hy Gardner and asked him to meet me at
the Blue Ribbon with anything he might have on Torrence.
All he said was, "Now what?" But it meant he'd be
there.

He showed up with Pete Ladero, who did legwork for
a political columnist, and over lunch I picked out all
the information on Torrence I could get. Substantially,
it was the same as the better magazines had reported.
Sim Torrence was a product of New York schools,
had graduated *magna cum laude* and gone into public
service immediately afterward. He had a small inheritance
that made him independent enough to be able to afford
the work and a determination that took him from an
assistant D.A. through the main office into the State
Legislature and Senate, and now he was standing at

the threshold of the governorship. I said, "What's wrong with the guy?"

"Nothing," Pete told me. "Find out something and I'll peddle it to the opposition for a million bucks."

"Didn't they try?"

"You kidding?"

Hy shoved his glasses up on his forehead. "So what's the business then, Mike? What are you laying into Torrence for?"

"Curiosity right now. His name came up in a little deal a while back."

"This for publication?"

"No. It's strictly for curiosity value."

"I wish to hell you'd say what you're going to say."

"Okay," I agreed. "What about his marriage?"

Pete and Hy looked at each other, shrugged, and Pete said, "His wife died years ago. He never remarried."

"Who was she?"

Pete thought a moment, then: "Her name was Devon, Sally Devon. If I remember right she was a fairly pretty showgirl when it was fashionable to marry showgirls. But hell, she died not long after the war. There was never any scandal connected with his marriage."

"What about the kid?" I asked.

Pete shook his head. "Nothing. I've met her several times. Torrence adopted her when her mother died, sent her to pretty good schools, and she's lived with him since."

"She ran away."

"You don't run away when you're over twenty-one," he reminded me. "Sim probably has given her a checking account that will keep her provided for wherever she goes." He paused a moment. "I don't get the angle there."

"Because I haven't got one," I said. "In my business names and people get dropped into funny places and no matter who they are they get checked out. Hell, it never hurts to prove a clean man clean."

Pete agreed with a nod, finished his coffee, and told us so-long. Hy said, "Satisfied?"

"I'm getting there."

"Do I get a hint at least?"

"Sure. The two dead men the night I found Velda."

Hy frowned and pulled his glasses off, his cigar working across his mouth. "The ones who followed you and tried to nail Velda at the last minute?"

"That's the story the papers got, friend."

He waited, staring at me.

I said, "They had nothing to do with the espionage bit. They were part of another story."

"Brother!" Hy poked the cigar out in the ash tray and reached for his pencil and scratch sheets.

"No story yet, Hy. Hold it back. I'll tell you when."

Reluctantly, he put them back. "Okay, I'll wait."

"Velda had Torrence's kid with her. She took her in like a stray cat. Strictly coincidence, but there we are. The kid said she was hiding out from her old man, but whether she's lying or not, we know one thing: two dead men and a possible third say trouble's there."

"How the hell can you suppress stuff like that!" Hy exploded.

"Angles, buddy."

"Boy, you sure come on like Gangbusters. I hope you're protecting yourself."

"Don't worry about me."

"Don't worry, I won't."

Hy had to get back to his desk at the *Tribune* building so I dropped him off and went ahead to Pat's office. The uniformed sergeant at the desk waved to me, said Pat was upstairs in new quarters and to go ahead up.

He was eating at his desk as usual, too crammed with work to take time out at a lunch counter. But he wasn't too busy to talk to me. I was part of his work. He grinned and said, "How is Velda?"

"Fine, but not for you."

"Who knows?" He reached for the coffee container. "What's up?"

"What did you get on Levitt and the other guy?"

"Nothing new on Levitt. He'd been sporting some fresh money lately without saying where it came from. It was assumed that he picked up his old blackmail operations."

"And the other one?"

"Kid Hand. You knew him, didn't you?"

"I've seen him around. Small-time muscle."

"Then you haven't seen him lately. He's gone up in the world. Word has it that he's been handling all the bookie operations on the upper west side."

"Tillson's old run?"

"Hell, Tillson was knocked off a year ago."

"So who's Hand working for?"

"I wish I knew. Mr. Big has been given the innocuous-sounding name of Mr. Dickerson, but nobody seems to know any more about him."

"Somebody's going to be taking over Hand's end. There'll be a shake-up somewhere."

"Mike . . . you just don't know the rackets any more. It's all I.B.M.-style now. Business, purely business, and they're not being caught without a chain of command. No, there won't be a shake-up. It'll all happen nice and normally. Somebody else will be appointed to Kid Hand's job and that will be that."

"You guessed the bug, though, didn't you?"

Pat nodded. "Certainly. What's a wheel like Hand taking on a muscle job for anyway? You know the answer?"

"Sure. I'd say he was doing somebody a favor. Like somebody big."

"Yeah," Pat said sourly. "Now the question is, who was killing who? You nailed Hand, Levitt fired two shots, and we recovered one out of the ceiling."

"Another one got Hand's friend in the gut. You might check the hospitals."

"*Now* you tell me."

"Nuts, Pat. You figured it right after it happened."

He swung around idly in his chair, sipping at the coffee container. When he was ready he said, "What were they really after, Mike?"

I took my time too. "I don't know. Not yet I don't. But I'll find out."

"Great. And with all that top cover you got I have to sweat you out."

"Something like that."

"Let me clue you, Mike. We have a new Inspector. He's a tough nut and a smart one. Between him and the D.A., you're liable to find your tail in a jam. Right now they're trying hard to bust you loose for them to work over, so you'd better have pretty powerful friends in that office you seem to be working for."

27

I put my hat on and stood up. "Anything I come up with, you'll get."

"Gee, thanks," he said sarcastically, then grinned.

Sim Torrence lived inside a walled estate in Westchester that reflected the quiet dignity of real wealth and importance. A pair of ornate iron gates were opened wide, welcoming visitors, and I turned my rented Ford up the drive.

The house, a brick colonial type, was surrounded by blue spruces that reached to the eaves. Two black Caddies were parked in front of one wing and I pulled up behind them, got out, touched the doorbell, and waited.

I had expected a maid or a butler, but not a stunning brunette with electric blue eyes that seemed to spark at you. She had an early season tan that made her eyes and the red of her mouth jump right at you and when she smiled and said quizzically, "Yes?" it was like touching a hot line.

I grinned crookedly. "My name is Hammer. I'm looking for Mr. Torrence."

"Is he expecting you?"

"No, but I think he'll see me. It's about his daughter."

The eyes sparked again with some peculiar fear. "Is she . . . all right?"

"Fine."

Then relief took over and she held out her hand to me. "Please come in, Mr. Hammer. I'm Geraldine King, Mr. Torrence's secretary. He's going to be awfully glad to see you. Since Sue ran off again he's been so upset he can't do a thing."

"Again?"

She glanced up at me and nodded. "She's gone off several times before. If she only knew what she does to Mr. Torrence when she gets in one of her peeves she'd be more considerate. In here, Mr. Hammer." She pointed into a large study that smelled of cigars and old leather. "Make yourself at home, please."

There wasn't much time for that. Before I had a chance to make a circuit of the room I heard the sound of hurried feet and Big Sim Torrence, the Man-Most-Likely-To-Succeed, came in looking not at all like a politician, but with the genuine worry of any distraught father.

He held out his hand, grabbed mine, and said, "Thanks for coming, Mr. Hammer." He paused, offered me a chair, and sat down. "Now, where is Sue? Is she all right?"

"Sure. Right now she's with a friend of mine."

"Where, Mr. Hammer?"

"In the city."

He perched on the edge of the chair and frowned. "She . . . *does* intend to come back here?"

"Maybe."

His face hardened then. It was a face that had an expression I had seen a thousand times in courtrooms. It became a prosecuting attorney's face who suddenly found himself with a hostile witness and was determined to drag out the right answers the hard way.

Torrence said, "Perhaps I don't understand your concern in this matter."

"Perhaps not. First, let me tell you that it's by accident that I'm here at all. Sue was sort of taken in hand by my secretary and I made a promise to look into things before letting her return."

"Oh?" He looked down into his hands. "You are . . . qualified for this matter then?"

The wallet worked it magic again and the hostility faded from his face. His expression was serious, yet touched with impatience. "Then please get to the point, Mr. Hammer. I've worried enough about Sue so . . ."

"It's simple enough. The kid says she's scared stiff of you."

A look of pain flitted across his eyes. He held up his hand to stop me, nodded, and looked toward the window. "I know, I know. She says I killed her mother."

He caught me a little off base. When he looked around once more I said, "That's right."

"May I explain something?"

"I wish somebody would."

Torrence settled back in his chair, rubbing his face with one hand. His voice was flat, as though he had gone through the routine countless times before. "I married Sally Devon six months after her husband died.
29

Sue was less than a year old at the time. I had known Sally for years then and it was like . . . well, we were old friends. What I didn't know was that Sally had become an alcoholic. In the first years of our marriage she grew worse in spite of everything we tried to do. Sally took to staying at my place in the Catskills with an old lady for a housekeeper, refusing to come into the city, refusing any help . . . just drinking herself to death. She kept Sue with her although it was old Mrs. Lee who really took care of the child. One night she drank herself into a stupor, went outside into the bitter cold for something, and passed out. She was unconscious when Mrs. Lee found her and dead before either a doctor or I could get to her. For some reason the child thinks I had something to do with it."

"She says her mother told her something before she died."

"I know that too. She can't recall anything, but continues to make the charge against me." He paused and rubbed his temples. "Sue has been a problem. I've tried the best schools and let her follow her own desires but nothing seems to help matters any. She wants to be a showgirl like her mother was." He looked up at me slowly. "I wish I knew the answer."

This time I was pretty direct. "She says you're trying to kill her."

His reaction was one of amazement. *"What?"* Very slowly he came to the edge of his seat. *"What's that?"*

"A car tried to run her down, she was deliberately followed, and somebody took a shot at her."

"Are you sure?"

"I am about the last time. I was there when it happened." I didn't bother giving him any of the details.

"But . . . why haven't I heard . . . ?"

"Because it involved another matter too. In time you'll hear about it. Not now. Just let's say it happened."

For the first time his courtroom composure left him. He waved his hands like a lost person and shook his head.

I said, "Mr. Torrence, do you have any enemies?"

"Enemies?"

"That's right."

"I . . . don't think so." He reflected a moment and

went on. "Political enemies, perhaps. There are two parties and . . ."

"Would they want to kill you?" I interrupted.

"No . . . certainly not. Disagree, but that's all."

"What about women?" I asked bluntly.

He paid no attention to my tone. "Mr. Hammer . . . I haven't kept company with a woman since Sally died. This is a pretty well-known fact."

I looked toward the door meaningfully. "You keep pretty company."

"Geraldine King was assigned to me by our state chairman. She has been with me through three political campaigns. Between times she works with others in the party running for office."

"No offense," I said. "But how about other possibles? Could you have made any special enemies during your political career?"

"Again, none that I know of who would want to kill me."

"You were a D.A. once."

"That was twenty-some years ago."

"So go back that far."

Torrence shrugged impatiently. "There were a dozen threats, some made right in the courtroom. Two attempts that were unsuccessful."

"What happened?"

"Nothing," he said. "Police routine stopped the action. Both persons were apprehended and sent back to prison. Since then both have died, one of T.B., the other of an ulcer."

"You kept track of them?"

"No, the police did. They thought it best to inform me. I wasn't particularly worried."

"Particularly?"

"Not for myself. For Sue and anyone else, yes. Personally, my recourse is to the law and the police. But remember this, Mr. Hammer, it isn't unusual for a District Attorney to be a target. There was a man named Dewey the mobs could have used dead, but to kill him would have meant that such pressure would be brought on organized crime that when Dutch Schultz wanted to kill him the mob killed Dutch instead. This is a precarious business and I realize it. At the same time,

31

I won't alter my own philosophies by conforming to standards of the scared."

"How often have you been scared?"

"Often. And you?"

"Too often, buddy." I grinned at him and he smiled back slowly, his eyes showing me he knew what I meant.

"Now about Sue."

"I'll speak to her."

"You'll bring her home?"

"That's up to Sue. I'll see what she says. Supposing she won't come?"

Torrence was silent a moment, thinking. "That's up to her then. She's a . . . child who isn't a child. Do you know what I mean?"

"Uh-huh."

He nodded. "She's well provided for financially and frankly, I don't see what else I can do for her. I'm at a point where I need advice."

"From whom?"

His eyes twinkled at me. "Perhaps from you, Mr. Hammer."

"Could be."

"May I ask your status first?"

"I hold a very peculiar legal authorization. At the moment it allows me to do damn near anything I want to. Within reason, of course."

"For how long?"

"You're quick, friend." He nodded and I said, "Until somebody cuts me out of it or I make a mistake."

"Oh?"

"And the day of mistakes is over."

"Then advise me. I need advice from someone who doesn't make mistakes any more." There was no sarcasm in his tone at all.

"I'll keep her with me until she wants out."

A full ten seconds passed before he thought it over, then he nodded, went to the other side of his desk and pulled out a checkbook. When he finished writing he handed me a pretty green paper made out for five thousand dollars and watched while I folded it lengthwise.

"That's pretty big," I said.

"Big men don't come little. Nor do big things. I

32

want Sue safe. I want Sue back. It's up to you now, Mr. Hammer. Where do you start?"

"By getting you to remember the name of the other guys who threatened to kill you."

"I doubt if those matters are of any importance."

"Suppose you let me do the deciding. A lot of trouble can come out of the past. A lot of dirt too. If you don't want me probing you can take your loot back. Then just for fun I might do it anyway."

"There's something personal about this with you, isn't there, Mr. Hammer? It isn't that you need the money or the practice. You needn't tell me, but there is something else."

We studied each other for the few ticks of time that it took for two pros in the same bit of business to realize that there wasn't much that could be hidden.

"You know me, Torrence."

"I know you, Mike. Doesn't everybody?"

I grinned and stuck the check in my pocket. "Not really," I said.

CHAPTER THREE

You can always make a start with a dead man. It's an ultimate end and a perfect beginning. Death is too definite to be ambiguous and when you deal with it your toes are in the chocks and not looking for a place to grab hold.

But death can be trouble too. It had been a long time and in seven years people could forget or stop worrying or rather play the odds and get themselves a name in the dark shadows of the never land of the night people.

Kid Hand was dead. Somebody would be mad. Somebody would be worried. By now everybody would know what happened in that tenement room and would be waiting. There would be those who remembered seven years ago and would wonder what came next. Some would know. Some would have to find out.

Me, maybe.

Off Broadway on Forty-ninth there's a hotel sandwiched in between slices of other buildings and on the street it has a screwy bar with a funny name filled with screwier people and even funnier names. They were new people, mostly, but some were still there after seven years and when I spotted Jersey Toby I nodded and watched him almost drop his beer and went to the bar and ordered a Four Roses and ginger.

The bartender was a silent old dog who mixed the drink, took my buck, and said, "Hello, Mike."

I said, "Hello, Charlie."

"You ain't been around."

"Didn't have to be."

"Glad you dumped the slop chutes."

"You hear too much."

"Bartenders like to talk too."

"To who?"

"Whom," he said.

"So whom?"

"Like other bartenders."

"Anybody else?"

"Nobody else," he said gently.

34

"Business is business," I grinned.

"So be it, Mike."

"Sure, Charlie," I told him.

He walked away and set up a couple for the hookers working the tourist traffic at the other end, then sort of stayed in the middle with a small worried expression on his face. Outside it was hot and sticky and here it was cool and quiet with the dramatic music of Franck's Symphony in D Minor coming through the stereo speakers too softly to be as aggressive as it should. It could have been a logical place for anybody to drop in for a break from the wild city outside.

One of the hookers spotted my two twenties on the bar and broke away from her tourist friend long enough to hit the cigarette machine behind me. Without looking around she said, "Lonely?"

I didn't look around either. "Sometimes."

"Now?"

"Not now," I said.

She turned around, grinned, and popped a butt in her pretty mouth. "Crazy native," she said.

"A real aborigine."

She laughed down in her throat. "So back to the flatland foreigners."

Jersey Toby waited until she left, then did the cigarette-machine bit himself before taking his place beside me. He made it look nice and natural, even to getting into a set routine of being a sudden bar friend and buying a drink.

When the act was over he said, "Look, Mike . . ."

"Quit sweating, buddy."

"You come for me or just anybody?"

"Just anybody."

"I don't like it when you don't come on hard."

"A new technique, Toby."

"Knock it off, Mike. Hell, I know you from the old days. You think I don't know what happened already?"

"Like what?"

"Like what's with Levitt and Kid Hand. You got rocks in your head? You think you can come shooting into the city any more? Man, things ain't like before. You been away and you should've stayed away. Now before you get me involved, let me tell you one big thing.

35

Don't make me out a patsy. I ain't telling you nothing. Not one goddamn thing. Lay off me. I been doing a lot of small-time crap that don't get me no heat from either direction and that's the way I like it."

"Great."

"And no soft stuff too. Save that bull for the enlisted men."

"What are you pitching now?"

"I'm a pimp."

"You came down in the world."

"Yeah? Well maybe I did, but I got bucks going for me now and a couple of broads who like the bit. I do it square and not like some of the creeps and on top there's enough juice to pay off who needs paying off, like. Y'know?"

"I won't eat your bread, kiddo."

"Goddamn right."

He sat there glowering into his drink, satisfied that he had made his point, then I reached over and took his hand and held it against my side where the .45 was strung and said, "Remember?"

When he took his hand back he was shaking. "You're still nuts," he said. "You ain't nothing no more. One push with that rod and you've had it. I'm still paying juice."

This time I pulled the other cork. I took out the wallet and opened it like I was going to put my money back only I let him see the card in the window. He took a good look, his eyes going wide, then reached for his drink. "An ace, Toby," I said. "Now do we go to your place or my place?"

"I got a room upstairs," he told me.

"Where?"

"313."

"Ten minutes. You take off first."

It was a back-alley room that had the antiseptic appearance of all revamped hotel rooms, but still smelled of stale beer, old clothes, and tired air. Jersey Toby opened a beer for himself when I waved one off, then sat down with a resigned shrug and said, "Spill it, Mike."

"Kid Hand."

36

"He's dead."

"I know. I shot him. The top of his head came off and left a mess on the wall. He wasn't the first and he probably won't be the last."

Toby put the beer down slowly. *"You're nuts."*

"That's the best you can say?"

"No," he repeated. *"You're nuts.* I think you got a death wish."

"Toby . . ."

"I mean it, Mike. Like word goes around fast. You don't make a hit in this town without everybody knowing. You was crazy enough in those old days, but now you're real nuts. You think I don't know already? Hell, like everybody knows. I don't even want to be in the same room with you."

"You don't have a choice, Toby."

"Sure, so I'll pay later. So will you. Damn, Mike . . ."

"Kid Hand," I repeated.

"He took Tillson's job. Everybody knew about that."

"More."

"Like what, you nut! How the hell should I know about Kid? We ain't in the same game. I'm pimping. You know what he was? Like a big shot! Mr. Dickerson's right-hand boy. You think I'm going to . . . ?"

"Who?"

"Knock it off . . . you know."

"Who, Toby?"

"Mr. Dickerson."

"Who he, buddy?"

"Mike . . ."

"Don't screw around with me."

"Okay. So who knows from Dickerson? He's the new one in. He's the big one. He comes in with power and all the hard boys are flocking back. Hell, man, I can't tell you more. All I know is Mr. Dickerson and he's the gas."

"Political?"

"Not him, you nut. This one's power. Like firepower, man. You know what's happening in this town? They're coming in from the burgs, man. Bit shooters and they're gathering around waiting for orders. I feel the stream going by but I ain't fishing. Too long the mobs have

37

been dead . . . now it's like Indians again. A chief is back and the crazy Soos is rejoicing. That's all I can say."

"Kid Hand?"

"Crazy, man. A shooter and he knew where his bread was. He was on the way up until he decided to get back in the ranks again. He should've stayed where he was."

"Why?"

"Why what?"

"He pulled on me. I don't take that crap."

"He knew it was you, maybe? He knew it was anybody?"

"Somebody said he might have been doing a personal favor."

Toby got up and faced the blank window. "Sure, why not? Favors are important. It makes you look big. It proves like you're not a punk. It proves . . ."

"It proves how fast you can get killed, too."

Slowly, he turned around. "Am I in the middle, Mike?"

"I don't see how."

"Ask it straight."

"Who is Dickerson?"

"Nobody knows. Just that he's big."

"Money?"

"I guess."

"Who takes Kid Hand's place?"

"Whoever can grab it. I'd say Del Penner. He's pretty tough. He had a fall ten years ago, but came back to grab off the jukes in Chi, then moved into the bolita and hi-li in Miami. He was pushing Kid pretty hard."

"Then maybe Kid's move in on me was part of a power grab."

"Favors don't hurt nobody."

"It killed Kid."

"So he didn't know it was you."

I looked at him a long time, then his face got tight and he turned away. When he gulped down his beer he looked at me, shrugged, and said, "Word goes it was a personal favor. You were a surprise. You just don't know what kind of a surprise. It wasn't with you. It was something else. That's all. I don't know . . . I don't want to know. Let me make my bucks my own way, only stay loose, man."

"Why?"

38

"You're hot now, man. Everybody knows. Everybody's looking."

"I've had heat before."

"Not like this." He looked into his beer, shrugged, and decided. "You ever hear of Marv Kania?"

"No."

"He's a contract man from St. Loo. Punk about twenty-eight, got a fall for murder second when he was a teen-ager, joined with Pax in K.C., then did the route with Arnold Philips on the coast and back to St. Loo. They figured he was a contract kill on Shulburger, Angelo, and Vince Pago and the big Carlysle hit in L.A. He's got plenty of cover and is as nuts as you are."

"What does that make me, Toby?"

"A target, man. He's in town with a slug in his gut and everybody knows how it happened. If he dies you're lucky. If he don't you're dead."

I got up and put on my hat. "My luck's been pretty good lately," I said.

He nodded gravely. "I hope it holds."

When I went to open the door he added, "Maybe I don't, too."

"Why?"

"I don't want to be around when it stops. You'll make an awful splash."

"It figures."

"Sure it does," he said.

Then I went back to her, the beautiful one whose hair hung dark and long, whose body was a quiet concert in curves and colors of white and shadow that rose softly under a single sheet into a woman's fulfillment of mounded breasts and soft clefts.

She didn't hear me come in until I said, "Velda . . ."

Then her eyes opened, slowly at first, then with the startled suddenness of a deer awakened and her hand moved and I knew what she had in it. When she knew it was me her fingers relaxed, came out from under the cover, and reached for mine.

"You can lose that way, kid," I said.

"Not when you're here."

"It wasn't always me."

"This is *now*, Mike," she said. It was almost me thinking
39

again when I walked up the steps a couple of days ago.

I took her hand, then in one full sweep flipped the sheet off her body and looked at her.

What is it when you see woman naked? *Woman.* Long. Lovely. Tousled. Skin that looks slippery in the small light. Pink things that are the summit. A wide, shadowy mass that is the crest. Desire that rests in the soft fold of flesh that can speak and taste and tell that it wants you with the sudden contractions and quickening intake of breath. A mouth that opens wetly and moves with soundless words of love.

I sat on the edge of the bed and let my fingers explore her. The invitation had always been there, but for the first time it was accepted. Now I could touch and feel and enjoy and know that this was mine. She gasped once, and said, "Your eyes are crazy, Mike."

"You can't see them."

"But I know. They're wild Irish brown green and they're crazy."

"I know."

"Then do what I want."

"Not me, Kid. You're only a broad and I do what I want."

"Then do it."

"Are you ready?" I asked.

"I've always been ready."

"No you haven't."

"I am now."

Her face was turned toward mine, the high planes in her cheeks throwing dark shades toward her lips, her eyes bright with a strange wetness, and when I bent forward and kissed her it was like tasting the animal wildness of a tiger filled with an insensate hunger that wanted to swallow its victim whole and I knew what woman was like. Pure woman.

Across the room, muffled because of the alcove, came a peculiar distant tone that made the scales, rising and falling with an eerie quality that had a banshee touch, and Velda said, "She's awake."

I pulled the sheet up and tucked it around her shoulders. "She isn't."

"We can go somewhere."

"No. The biggest word."

"Mike . . ."

"First we get rid of the trouble. It won't be right until then."

I could feel her eyes. "With you there will always be trouble."

"Not this trouble."

"Haven't we had enough?"

I shook my head. "Some people it's always with. You know me now. It comes fast, it lasts awhile, then it ends fast."

"You never change, do you?"

"Kitten, I don't expect to. Things happen, but they never change."

"Will it be us?"

"It has to be. In the meantime there are things to do. You ready?"

She grinned at me, the implication clear. "I've always been ready. You just never asked before."

"I never ask. I take."

"Take."

"When I'm ready. Not now. Get up."

Velda was a woman. She slid out of bed and dressed, deliberately, so I could watch everything she did, then reached into the top drawer of the dresser and pulled out a clip holster and slid it inside her skirt, the slide going over the wide belt she wore. The flat-sided Browning didn't even make a bulge.

I said, "If anybody ever shot me with that I'd tear their arms off."

"Not if you got shot in the head," she told me.

I called Rickerby from downstairs and he had a man stand by while we were gone. Sue was asleep, I thought, but I couldn't be sure. At least she wasn't going anyplace until we got back. We walked to the parking lot where I picked up the rented Ford and cut over to the West Side Highway.

She waited until I was on the ramp to ask, "Where are we going?"

"There's a place called 'The Angus Bull.' It's a new one for the racket boys."

"Who told you?"

"Pat."

41

"And whom do I con?"

"A man named Del Penner. If he isn't there you'll pick up a lead if you work it right. He was pushing Kid Hand and will probably take his place in the group. What you want to know is this . . . who is Mr. Dickerson?"

She threw me a funny glance and I filled her in on the small details. I watched her out of the corner of my eyes while she picked it all apart and put it back together again. There was something new about her now that wasn't there seven years ago. Then she had been a secretary, a girl with her own P.I. ticket and the right to carry a gun. Then she had been a girl with a peculiar past I hadn't known about. Now she was a woman, still with a peculiar past and a gun, but with a strange new subtlety added that was nurtured during those years behind the Iron Curtain in the biggest chase scene civilization had ever known.

"Where do we clear?"

"Through Pat."

"Or your friend Rickerby?"

"Keep him as an alternate. It isn't his field yet, so we'll stay local."

"Where will you be?"

"Running down the immediate past of a guy called Basil Levitt. Pat came up with nothing. They're still on the job, but he had no office and no records. Whatever he carried he carried in his hat, but he sure was working for somebody. He was after you and the kid and was four days watching your joint. I don't know what we have going, but these are the only leads we have."

"There's Sue."

"She has nothing to say yet."

"Did you believe what she said about her father trying to kill her?"

"No."

"Why not?"

"Because it isn't logical. The kid's a neurotic type and until something proves out I'm not going along with childish notions."

"Two dead men aren't notions."

"There's more to it than that, baby. Let me do it my way, okay?"

"Sure. It's always your way, isn't it?"

"Sure."

"Is that why I love you?"

"Sure."

"And you love me because I think that way?"

"Why sure."

"I'm home, Mike."

I touched her knee and felt her leg harden. "You never were away, kid."

She was on her own when I dropped her downtown. She grinned at me, waved, and I let her go. There was something relaxing about the whole thing now. No more tight feeling in the gut. No more of that big empty hole that was her. She was there and bigger than ever, still with the gun on her belt and ready to follow.

Going through Levitt's place was only a matter of curiosity. It was a room, nothing more. The landlady said he had been there six months and never caused trouble, paid his rent, and she didn't want to talk to any more cops. The neighbors didn't know anything about him at all and didn't want to find out. The local tavern owner had never served him and couldn't care less. But up in his room the ash trays had been full of butts and there were two empty cartons in the garbage and anyone who smokes that much had to pick up cigarettes somewhere.

Basil Levitt did it two blocks away. He got his papers there too. The old lady who ran the place remembered him well and didn't mind talking about it.

"I know the one," she told me. "I wondered when the cops would get down here. I even woulda seen them only I wanted to see how fast they'd get here. Sure took you long enough. Where you from, son?"

"Uptown."

"You know what happened?"

"Not yet."

"So what do you want with me?"

"Just talk, Mom."

"So ask."

"Suppose you tell." I grinned at her. "Maybe you want the third degree, sweetie, just like in TV . . . okay?"

She waved her hand at me. "That stuff is dead. Who

43

hits old ladies any more except deliquents?"

"Me. I hit old ladies."

"You look like the type. So ask me."

"Okay . . . any friends?"

She shook her head. "No, but he makes phone calls. One of the hot boys . . . never shuts the door." She nodded toward the pay booth in back.

"You listened?"

"Why not? I'm too old to screw so I get a kick out of love talk."

"How about that?"

"Yeah, how?" She smiled crookedly and opened herself a Coke. "He never talked love talk, never. Just money and always mad."

"More, Mom."

"He'd talk pretty big loot. Five G's was the last . . . like he was a betting man. Was he, son?"

"He bet his skin and lost. Now more."

She made a gesture with her shoulders. "Last time he was real mad. Said something was taking too long and wanted more loot. I don't think he got it."

"Any names?"

"Nope. He didn't call somebody's house, either."

I waited and she grinned broadly.

"He only called at a certain time. ⊶ had to speak up like wherever the other party was, it was damn noisy. That's how come I heard him."

"You'd make a good cop, Mom."

"I been around long enough, son. You want to know something else?"

"That's what I'm here for."

"He carried a package once. It was all done up in brown paper and it wasn't light. It was a gun. Rifle all taken down, I'd say. You like that bit?"

"You're doing great. How'd you know?"

"Easy. It *clunked* when he set it down. Besides, I could smell the gun oil. My old man was a nut on those things before he kicked off. I smelled that stuff around the house for years."

Then I knew what bugged me right after Basil Levitt died. I said my thanks and turned to go. She said, "Hey . . ."

"What?"

"Would you really hit an old lady?"

I grinned at her. "Only when they need it," I said.

I stood in the room that had been Velda's and scanned the other side of the street. It didn't take long to sort out the only windows that were set right for an ambush. Ten bucks to a fat old man got me the key with no questions asked and when I opened the door to the first one that was it.

The gun was an expensive sporting rifle with a load in the chamber, blocked in on a tripod screwed to a tabletop and the telescopic sights were centered on the same window I had looked out of a few minutes before. There were two empty cigarette cartons beside the gun, a tomato-juice can full of butts and spent matches, and the remains of a dozen sandwiches scattered around.

Basil's vigil had been a four-day one. For that long a time he had waited. At any time he could have had Velda. He knew she was there. He told me so. He had watched her that long but couldn't move in.

The reason for his wait was plain now. It wasn't her he was after at all. It was the kid. He wanted her. He was on a contract to knock her off and had to wait for her to show.

Only she didn't. Velda had kept her upstairs out of sight. It was only when I came on the scene that he had to break his pattern. He didn't know why I was there but couldn't take any chances. I might be after the same target he was after but for a different reason: to get her out.

So now it was back to the little Lolita-type again.

CHAPTER FOUR

It had been a long time since I had seen Joey Adams and his wife Cindy. Now, besides doing his major night-club routines with time off for tent-circus Broadway musicals and world-wide junkets, he was president of AGVA. But he hadn't changed a bit. Neither had Cindy. She was still her same stunning self in the trademark colors of scarlet and midnight whamming out a column for *TV Guide*.

I told the girl not to announce me and when I went in Joey was perched on the edge of his desk trying to talk Cindy out of something new in minks. He wasn't getting anywhere. I said, "Hello, buddy."

He looked over his shoulder, grinned, and hopped off the desk with his hand out. "I'll be damned," he said, "you finally picked up the rain check. Where you been?"

"On the wrong street." I looked past him. "Hello, beautiful."

Cindy threw me a flashing smile. "I told Joey you'd show up. We've been following the obituaries. You leave a trail, Mike."

"I was following one."

"That's what Hy said. You big fink, why didn't you come visit when you needed help?"

"Hell, kid, I didn't need any help to stay drunk."

"That's not what I meant."

Joey waved at her impatiently. "Come on, come on, what's new? Look, suppose we . . ."

"I need help now, pal."

It caught him off balance a second. "Listen, I'm no AA, but . . ."

"Not that kind of help," I grinned.

"Oh?"

"You've been bugging me to play cop for how long, Joey?"

His eyes lit up like a marquee but Cindy got there first.

"Listen, old friend, you keep my boy away from the shooters. Like he's mine and I want to keep him in one piece. He's just a comedian and those gun routines are hard on the complexion."

"Cut it out, Cindy. If Mike wants . . ."

"Don't sweat it, friend. Just a simple favor."

He looked disappointed.

"But it's something you can get to where I can't," I added.

Joey laughed and faked a swing at my gut. "So name it, kid."

"How far back do your files go?"

"Well," he shrugged, "what do you want to know?"

I sat on the edge of the desk and lined things up in my mind. "There was a showgirl named Sally Devon who was in business over twenty years ago. Name mean anything?"

Joey squinted and shook his head. "Should it?"

"Not necessarily. I doubt if she was a headliner."

"Mike . . ." Cindy uncoiled from her chair and stood beside Joey. "Wasn't she Sim Torrence's wife at one time?"

I nodded.

"How'd you know?" Joey asked.

"I'm just clever."

"What do you know about her, honey?"

"Nothing at all, but I happened to be talking politics to one of Joey's friends and he dropped her name in the hat. He had worked with her at one time."

"Now she's in politics," Joey grunted. "So who were you talking to?"

"Bert Reese."

"What do you think, Joey? Do a rundown for me? Maybe Bert can steer you to somebody else that would know about her."

"Sure, but if it's politics you want, Cindy can . . ."

"It's not politics. Just get a line on her show-biz activities. She would've been in from twenty to thirty years back. Somebody at Equity might know her or the old chorus-line bunch. She was married to Sim Torrence while he was still a small-timer so the connection might bring somebody's memory back. Seem possible?"

"Sure, Mike, sure. The kids always keep in touch. They never forget. Hell, you know show business. I'll dig around."

"How long will it take?"

"I ought to have something by tomorrow. Where'll I get in touch?"

"My old office. I'm back in business, or reach me through the Blue Ribbon Restaurant."

He gave me that big grin again and winked. Now he was doing an act he liked. There are always frustrated cops and firemen. I shook hands with Joey, waved at Cindy, and left them to battle about the mink bit again.

Rickerby's man gave me a funny look and a curt nod when I showed, asked if there were anything else, and when I said no, made his phone call to clear and took off. Then I went upstairs.

I could hear her all the way, like a wild bird singing a crazy melody. She had an incredible range to her voice and just let it go, trilling some strange tune that had a familiar note, but was being interpreted out of its symphonic character.

The singing didn't come from the floor where I had left her, either. It was higher up and I made the last flight in a rush and stood at the end of the corridor with the .45 in my hand wondering what the hell was going on. She had everything wrapped up in that voice, fear, hate, anxiety, but no hope at all.

When I pushed the door open slowly her voice came flooding out from the peculiar echo chamber of the empty room. She stood facing the corner, both hands against the wall, her head down, her shoulders weaving gently with the rhythm of her voice, her silken blonde hair a gold reflection from the small bulb overhead.

I said, "Sue . . ." and she turned slowly, never stopping, but, seeing me there, went into a quiet ballet step until she stopped and let her voice die out on a high lilting note. There was something gone in her eyes and it took a half minute for her to realize just who I was.

"What are you doing up here?"

"It's empty," she said finally.

"Why do you want it like that?"

48

She let her hands drift behind her back. "Furniture looks at you. It means people and I don't want any people."

"Why, Sue?"

"They hurt you."

"Did somebody hurt you?"

"You know."

"I know that nobody has hurt you so far."

"So far. They killed my mother."

"You don't know that."

"Yes I do. A snake killed her."

"A what?"

"A snake."

"Your mother died of natural causes. She was . . . a sick woman."

This time Sue shook her head patiently. "I've been remembering. She was afraid of a snake. She told me so. She said it was the snake."

"You were too young to remember."

"No I wasn't."

I held out my hand to her and she took it. "Let's go downstairs, sugar. I want to talk to you."

"All right. Can I come back up here when I want to?"

"Sure. No trouble. Just don't go outside."

Those big brown eyes came up to mine with a sudden hunted look. "You know somebody wants to hurt me too, don't you?"

"Okay, kid, I won't try to con you. Maybe it will make you a little cautious. I think somebody is after you. Why, I don't know, but stick it out the way I tell you to, all right?"

"All right, Mike."

I waited until she had finished her coffee before I dropped the bomb on her. I said, "Sue . . ."

Then her eyes looked up and with a sudden intuition she knew what I was going to say.

"Would you mind going home?"

"I won't go," she said simply.

"You want to find out what really happened to your mother, don't you?"

She nodded.

"You can help if you do what I ask."

49

"How will that help?"

"You got big ears, kid. I'm an old soldier who knows his way around this business and you just don't fool me, baby. You can do anything you want to. Go back there and stay with it. Somebody wants you nailed, sugar, and if I can get you in a safe place I can scrounge without having you to worry about."

Sue smiled without meaning and looked down at her hands. "*He* wants me dead."

"Okay, we'll play it your way. *If* he does there's nothing he can do about it now. There're too many eyes watching you."

"Are yours, Mike?"

I grinned. "Hell, I can't take 'em off you."

"Don't fool with me, Mike."

"All right, Sue. Now listen. Your old man paid me five grand to handle this mess. It isn't like he's caught in a trap and is trying to con me because he knows all about me. I'm no mouse. I've knocked over too many punks and broke too many big ones to play little-boy games with."

"Are you *really* convinced, Mike?"

"Honey, until it's all locked up, tight, I'm never convinced, but at this stage we have to work the angles. Now, will you go back?"

She waited a moment, then looked up again. "If you want me to."

"I want you to."

"Will I see you again?"

Those big brown eyes were a little too much. "Sure, but what's a guy like me going to do with a girl like you?"

A smile touched her mouth. "Plenty, I think," she said.

Sim Torrence was out, but Geraldine King made the arrangements for a limousine to pick up Sue. I waited for it to arrive, watched her leave, then went back to my office. I got out at the eighth floor, edged around the guy leaning up against the wall beside the buttons with his back to me, and if it didn't suddenly occur to me that his position was a little too awkward to be normal and that he might be sick I never would have turned around and I would have died face down on the marble floor.

I had that one split-second glance at a pain- and hate-contorted face before I threw myself back toward the wall scratching for the .45 when his gun blasted twice and both shots rocketed off the floor beside my face.

Then I had the .45 out and ready but it was too late. He had stepped back into the elevator I had just left and the doors were closing. There wasn't any sense chasing him. The exit stairs were down the far end of the corridor and the elevator was a quick one. I got up, dusted myself off, and looked up at the guy who stuck his head out of a neighboring door. He said, "What was that?"

"Be damned if I know. Sounded like it was in the elevator."

"Something's always happening to that thing," he said passively, then closed his door.

Both slugs were imbedded in the plaster at the end of the hall, flattened at the nose and scratched, but with enough rifling marks showing for the lab to make something out of it. I dropped them in my pocket and went to my office. I dialed Pat, told him what had happened, and heard him let out a short laugh. "You're still lucky, Mike. For how long?"

"Who knows?"

"You recognize him?"

"He's the guy Basil Levitt shot, buddy. I'd say his name was Marv Kania."

"Mike . . ."

"I know his history. You got something out on him?"

"For a month. He's wanted all over. You sure about this?"

"I'm sure."

"He must want you pretty badly."

"Pat, he's got a bullet in him. He's not going to last like he is and if he's staying alive it's to get me first. If we can nail him we can find out what this is all about. If he knows he's wanted he can't go to a doctor and if he knows he's dying he'll do anything to come at me again. Now damn it, a shot-up guy can't go prancing around the streets, you know that."

51

"He's doing it."

"So he'll fall. Somebody'll try to help him and he'll nail them too. He just can't follow me around, I move too fast."

"He'll wait you out, Mike."

"How?"

"You're not thinking straight. If he knows what this operation is about he'll know where you'll be looking sooner or later. All he has to do is wait there."

"What about in the meantime?"

"I'll get on it right away. If he left a trail we'll find it. There aren't too many places he can hole up."

"Okay."

"And, buddy . . ."

"What, Pat?"

"Hands off if you nail him, understand? I got enough people on my back right now. This new D.A. is trying to break your license."

"Can he?"

"It can be done."

"Well hell, tell him I'm cooperating all the way. If you look in the downstairs apartment in the building across the street from where Velda was staying you'll find a sniper's rifle that belonged to Basil Levitt. Maybe you can backtrack that."

"Now you tell me," he said softly.

"I just located it."

"What does it mean?"

I didn't tell him what I thought at all. "Got me. You figure it out."

"Maybe I will. Now you get those slugs down to me as fast as you can."

"By messenger service right now."

When I hung up I called Arrow, had a boy pick up the envelope with the two chunks of lead, got them off, then stretched out on the couch.

I slept for three hours, a hard, tight sleep that was almost dreamless, and when the phone went off it didn't awaken me until the fourth or fifth time. When I said hello, Velda's voice said, "Mike . . ."

"Here, kitten. What's up?"

"Can you meet me for some small talk, honey?"

My fingers tightened involuntarily around the receiver. *Small talk* was a simple code. *Trouble*, it meant, *be careful.*

In case somebody was on an extension I kept my voice light. "Sure, kid. Where are you?"

"A little place on Eighth Avenue near the Garden . . . Lew Green's Bar."

"I know where it is. Be right down."

"And, Mike, . . . come alone."

"Okay."

On the way out I stopped by Nat Drutman's office and talked him out of a .32 automatic he kept in his desk, shoved it under my belt behind my back, and grabbed a cab for Lew Green's Bar. There was a dampness in the air and a slick was showing on the streets, reflecting the lights of the city back from all angles. It was one of those nights that had a bad smell to it.

Inside the bar a pair of chunkers were swapping stories in a half-drunken tone while a TV blared from the wall. A small archway led into the back room that was nestled in semi-darkness and when I went in a thin, reedy voice said from one side, "Walk easy, mister."

He had his hands in his side pockets and would have been easy to take, loaded or not, but I went along with him. He steered me past the booths to the side entrance where another one waited who grinned in an insolent way and said, "He carries a heavy piece. You look for it?"

"You do it," the thin guy said.

He knew right where to look. He dragged the .45 out, said, "Nice," grinned again, and stuck it in his pocket. "Now outside. We got transportation waiting. You're real V.I.P."

The place they took me to was in Long Island City, a section ready to be torn down to make way for a new factory building. The car stopped outside an abandoned store and when the smart one nodded I followed him around the back with the thin one six feet behind me and went on inside.

They sat at a table, three of them, with Velda in a chair at the end. A single Coleman lamp threw everything into sharp lights and shadows, making their faces look unreal.

I looked past them to Velda. "You okay, honey?"

She nodded, but there was a tight cast to her mouth.

The heavy-set guy in the homburg said, "So you're Mike Hammer."

I took a wild guess. "Del Penner."

His face hardened. "He clean?"

Both the guys at the door behind him nodded and the one took my .45 out and showed it. Del said, "You came too easy, Hammer."

"Who expected trouble?"

"In your business you should always expect it."

"I'll remember it. What's the action, Penner?"

"You sent her asking about me. Why?"

"Because I'm getting my toes stepped on. A guy named Kid Hand got shot and I hear you're taking his place. I don't like to get pushed. Now what?"

"You'll get more than pushed, Hammer. Word's around that you got yourself some top cover and knocking you off can make too much noise. Not that it can't be handled, but who needs noise? Okay, you're after something, so spill it."

"Sure. You are stepping up then?"

Penner shrugged elaborately. "Somebody takes over. What else?"

"Who's Dickerson?"

Everybody looked at everybody else before Del Penner decided to answer me. He finally made up his mind. "You know that much, then you can have this. *Nobody* knows who Mr. Dickerson is."

"Somebody knows."

"Maybe, but not you and not us. What else?"

"You pull this stunt on your own?"

"That you can bet your life on. When this broad started nosing around I wanted to know why. So I asked her and she told me. She said they were your orders. Now get this . . . I know about the whole schmear with you knocking off Kid Hand and getting Levitt bumped and leaving Marv Kania running around with a slug in his gut. I ain't got orders on you yet but like I said, when anybody noses around me I want to know why."

"Supposing I put it this way then, Penner. . . . I'm the same way. Anybody tries to shoot me up is in for a hard time. You looked like a good place to start with

54

and don't figure I'm the only one who'll think of it. You don't commit murder in this town and just walk away from it. If you're stepping into Kid Hand's job then you should know that too."

Penner smiled tightly. "The picture's clear, Hammer. I'm just stopping it before it gets started."

"Then this bit is supposed to be a warning?"

"Something like that."

"Or maybe you're doing a favor ahead of time."

"What's that mean?"

"Like Kid Hand was maybe doing a personal favor and stepped down off his pedestal to look like a big man."

The silence was tight. Del Penner just stared at me, not bothered at all by what I said. His hand reached up and touched his homburg and he sat back in his chair. "Warning then, Hammer. Don't make any more noise around me. I imagine you'd be about a fifteen-hundred-buck job. One thousand five hundred bucks can buy both of you dead and no mud on my hands. Clear?"

I put both hands on the table and leaned right into his face. "How much would you cost, Del?" I asked him. He glared at me, his eyes hard and bright. I said, "Come on, Velda. They're giving us a ride home."

We sat in the front next to the driver, the skinny guy in back. All the way into Manhattan he kept playing with my gun. When we got to my office the one behind the wheel said, "Out, mac."

"Let's have the rod."

"Nah, it's too good a piece for a punk like you. I want a souvenir."

So I put the .32 up against his neck while Velda swung around in her seat and pointed the automatic at the skinny guy and his whine was a tinny nasal sound he had trouble making. He handed over the .45 real easy, licking his lips and trying to say something. The one beside me said, "Look, mac . . ."

"I never come easy, buddy. You tell them all."

His eyes showed white all the way around and he knew. He knew all right. The car pulled away with a squeal of tires and I looked at Velda and laughed. "You play it that way by accident, honey?"

"I've had to read a lot of minds the past seven years. I knew how it would work. I just wanted you ready."

"I don't know whether to kiss you or smack your ass."

She grinned impishly. "You can *always* kiss me."

"Don't ask for it."

"Why not? It's the only way I'm going to get it, I think."

Teddy's place is a lush restaurant about as far downtown as it's possible to get without falling in the river. It seemed an unlikely spot for good food and celebrities, but there you got both. Hy Gardner was having a late supper with Joey and Cindy Adams, and when he spotted us, waved us over to the table.

Before we could talk he ordered up scampi and a steak for both of us, then: "You come down for supper or information?"

"Both."

"You got Joey really researching. He comes to me, I go to somebody else, and little by little I'm beginning to get some mighty curious ideas. When are you going to recite for publication?"

"When I have it where it should be."

"So what's the pitch on Sally Devon?"

"All yours, Joey," I said.

He could hardly wait to get it out. "Boy, what a deal you handed me. You threw an old broad my way. There was more dust on her records than a Joe Miller joke. Then you know who comes up with the answers?"

"Sure, Cindy."

"How'd you know?"

"Who else?"

"Drop dead. Anyway, we contacted some of the kids who worked with her only like now they're ready for the old ladies' home. Sure, she was in show business, but with her it didn't last long and was more of a front. Her old friends wouldn't say too much, being old friends and all, but you knew what they were thinking. Sally Devon was a high-priced whore. She ran with some of the big ones for a while, then got busted and wound up with some of the racket boys."

Velda looked at me, puzzled. "If she was involved

with the rackets, how'd she end up with Sim Torrence who was supposed to be so clean? That doesn't make sense."

"Sure it does," Hy told her. "He got her off a hook when he was still an assistant D.A. Look, she was still a beautiful doll then and you know the power of a doll. So they became friends. Later he married her. I can name a couple other top politicos who are married to women who used to be in the business. It isn't as uncommon as you think."

He put his fork down and sipped at his drink. "What do you make of it now?" When I didn't answer he said, "Blackmail?"

"I don't know," I admitted.

"Well, what else do you want?"

For a moment I sat there thinking. "Torrence is a pretty big wheel now, isn't he?"

"As big as they get without being in office."

"Okay, he said repeated threats were made on him by guys he helped put away."

"Ah, they all get that."

"They all don't have a mess like this either."

"So what?"

"This, Hy . . . I'd like a rundown on his big cases, on everyone who ever laid a threat on him. You ought to have that much in your morgue."

Hy shrugged and grinned at me. "I suppose you want it tonight."

"Why not?"

"So we'll finish the party in my office. Come on."

Hy's file on Sim Torrence was a thick one composed of hundreds of clippings. We all took a handful and found desk space to look them over. A little after one we had everything classified and cross-indexed. Joey had four cases of threats on Sim's life, Cindy had six, Velda and I both had three, and Hy one. He put all the clips in a Thermofax machine, pulled copies, handed them over, and put the files back.

"Now can we go home?" he said.

Joey wanted to go on with it until Cindy gave him a poke in the ribs.

"So let's all go home," I told him.

We said so-long downstairs and Velda and I headed

back toward the Stem. In the lower Forties I checked both of us into a hotel, kissed her at the door, and went down to my room. She didn't like it, but I still had work to do.

After a shower I sat on the bed and started through the clips. One by one I threw them all down until I had four left. All the rest who had threatened Sim Torrence were either dead or back in prison. Four were free, three on parole, and one having served a life sentence of thirty years.

Life.

Thirty years.

He was forty-two when he went in, seventy-two when he came out. His name was Sonny Motley and there was a picture of him in a shoe repair shop he ran on Amsterdam Avenue. I put the clips in the discard pile and looked at the others.

Sherman Buff, a two-time loser that Sim had put the screws to in court so that he caught a big fall. He threatened everybody including the judge, but Torrence in particular.

Arnold Goodwin who liked to be called Stud. Sex artist. Rapist. He put the full blame for his fall on Torrence, who not only prosecuted his case but processed it from the first complaint until his capture. No known address, but his parole officer could supply that.

Nicholas Beckhaus, burglar with a record who wound up cutting a cop during his capture. He and two others broke out of a police van during a routine transfer and it was Sim Torrence's office who ran him down until he was trapped in a rooming house. He shot a cop in that capture too. He promised to kill Torrence on sight when he got out. Address unknown, but he would have a parole officer too.

I folded the clips, put three in my pants pocket, and leaned back on the bed. Then there was a knock on the door.

I had the .45 in my hand, threw the bolt back, and moved to the side. Velda walked in grinning, closed the door, and stood there with her back against it. "Going to shoot me, Mike?"

"You crazy!"

"Uh-uh."

"What do you want?"

"You don't know?"

I reached out and pulled her in close, kissed her hair, then felt the fire of her mouth again. She leaned against me, her breasts firm and insistent against my naked chest, her body forming itself to mine.

"I'm going to treat you rough, my love . . . until you break down."

"You're going back to bed."

"To bed, yes, but not back." She smiled, pulled away, and walked to my sack. Little by little, slowly, every motion a time-honored motion, she took off her clothes. Then she stood there naked and smiling a moment before sliding into the bed where she lay there waiting.

"Let's see who's the roughest," I said, and lay down beside her. I punched out the light, got between the top sheet and the cover, turned on my side and closed my eyes.

"You big bastard," she said softly. "If I didn't love you I'd kill you."

CHAPTER FIVE

I was up and dressed before eight. The big, beautiful, tousled black-haired thing who had lain so comfortably against me all night stirred and looked at me through sleepy-lidded eyes, then stretched languidly and smiled.

"Frustrated?" I asked her.

"Determined." She stuck her tongue out at me. "You'll pay for last night."

"Get out of the sack. We have plenty to do."

"Watch."

I turned toward the mirror and put on my tie. "No, damn it."

But I couldn't help seeing her, either. It wasn't something you could take your eyes off very easily. She was too big, too lovely, her body a pattern of symmetry that was frightening. She posed deliberately, knowing I would watch her, then walked into the shower without bothering to close the door. And this time I saw something new. There was a fine, livid scar that ran diagonally across one hip and several parallel lines that traced themselves across the small of her back. I had seen those kind of marks before. Knives made them. Whips made them. My hands knotted up for a second and I yanked at my tie.

When she came out she had a towel wrapped sarong-fashion around her, smelling of soap and hot water, and this time I didn't watch her. Instead I pulled the clips out, made a pretense of reading them until she was dressed, gave them to her to keep in her handbag, and led her out the door.

At the elevator I punched the down button and put my hand through her arm. "Don't do that to me again, kitten."

Her teeth flashed through the smile. "Oh no, Mike. You've kept me waiting too long. I'll do anything to get you. You see . . . I'm not done with you yet. You can marry me right now or put up with some persecution."

"We haven't got time right now."

"Then get ready to suffer, gentleman." She gave my arm a squeeze and got on the elevator.

After breakfast I bypassed Pat's office to get a line on the parole officers handling Buff, Goodwin, and Beckhaus. Both Buff and Beckhaus were reporting to the same officer and he was glad to give me a rundown on their histories.

Sherman Buff was married, lived in Brooklyn, and operated a successful electronics shop that subcontracted jobs from larger companies. His address was good, his income sizable, and he had a woman he was crazy about and no desire to go back to the old life. The parole officer considered him a totally rehabilitated man.

Nicholas Beckhaus reported regularly, but he had to come in on the arm of his brother, a dentist, who supported him. At some time in prison he had been assaulted and his back permanently damaged so that he was a partial cripple. But more than that, there was brain damage too, so that his mental status was reduced to that of a ten-year-old.

The officer who handled Arnold Goodwin was more than anxious to talk about his charge. Goodwin had been trouble all the way and had stopped reporting in three months ago. Any information we could dig up on his whereabouts he'd appreciate. He was afraid of only one thing . . . that before Goodwin was found he'd kill somebody.

Arnold Goodwin looked like a good bet.

Velda said, "Did you want to see the other probable?"

"Sonny Motley?"

"It will only take a few minutes."

"He's in his seventies. Why?"

She moved her shoulders in thought. "He was a good story. The three-million-dollar killer."

"He wasn't in for murder. He was a three-time loser when they caught him in that robbery and he drew an automatic life sentence."

"That could make a man pretty mad," she reminded me.

"Sure, but guys in their seventies aren't going to hustle on a kill after thirty years in the pen. Be reasonable."

"Okay, but it wouldn't take long."

"Oh, hell," I said.

61

Sonny Motley's shoe repair shop had been open at seven as usual, the newsboy said, and pointed the place out to us. He was sitting in the window, a tired-looking old man bent over a metal foot a woman's shoe was fitted to, tapping on a heel. He nodded, peering up over his glasses at us like a shaven and partially bald Santa Claus.

Velda and I got up in the chairs and he put down his work to shuffle over to us, automatically beginning the routine of a shine. It wasn't a new place and the rack to one side of the machines was filled with completed and new jobs.

When he finished I gave him a buck and said, "Been here long?"

He rang the money up and smiled when I refused the change. "Year and a half." Then he pulled his glasses down a little more and looked at me closely. "Reporter?"

"Nope."

"Well, you look like a cop, but cops aren't interested in me any more. Not city cops. So that makes you independent, doesn't it?"

When I didn't answer him he chuckled. "I've had lots of experience with cops, son. Don't let it discourage you. What do you want to know?"

"You own this place?"

"Yup. Thirty years of saving a few cents a day the state paid me and making belts and wallets for the civilian trade outside bought me this. Really didn't cost much and it was the only trade I learned in the pen. But that's not what you want to know."

I laughed and nodded. "Okay, Sonny, it's about a promise you made a long time ago to kill Sim Torrence."

"Yeah, I get asked that lots of times. Mostly by reporters though." He pulled his stool over and squatted on it. "Guess I was pretty mad back then." He smiled patiently and pushed his glasses up. "Let's say that if he up and died I wouldn't shed any tears, but I'll tell you Mr. . . ."

"Hammer. Mike Hammer."

"Yes, Mr. Hammer . . . well, I'm just not about to go back inside walls again. Not that this is any different. Same work, same hours. But I'm on the outside. You understand?"

62

"Sure."

"Something else too. I'm old. I think different. I don't have those old feelings." He looked at Velda, then me. "Like with the women. Was a time when even thinking of one drove me nuts, knowing I couldn't have one. Oh, how I wanted to kill old Torrence then. But like I told you, once you get old the fire goes out and you don't care any more. Same way I feel about Torrence. I just don't care. Haven't even thought about him until somebody like you or a reporter shows up. Then I think of him and it gets funny. Sound silly to you?"

"Not so silly, Sonny."

He giggled and coughed, then looked up. "Silly like my name. Sonny. I was a heller with the women in them days. Looked young as hell and they loved to mother me. Made a lot of scores like that." For a moment his eyes grew dreamy, then he came back to the present. "Sonny. Ah, yeah, they were the days, but the fire is out now."

"Well . . ." I took Velda's arm and he caught the motion.

Eagerly, a man looking for company, he said, "If you want I could show you the papers on what happened. I had somebody save 'em. You wait here a minute." He got up, shuffled off through a curtained door, and we could hear him rummaging through his things. When he came back he laid out a pitiful few front pages of the old *World* and there he was spread all over the columns.

According to the testimony, in 1932 the Sonny Motley mob, with Black Conley second in command, were approached secretly by an unknown expert on heisting through an unrevealed medium. The offer was a beautifully engineered armored-car stickup. Sonny accepted and was given the intimate details of the robbery including facets known only to insiders which would make the thing come off.

Unfortunately, a young Assistant District Attorney named Sim Torrence got wind of the deal, checked it out, and with a squad of cops, broke up the robbery . . . but only after it had been accomplished. The transfer of three million dollars in cash had been made to a commandeered cab and in what looked like a spectacular double cross, or possibly an attempt to save his own skin, Black Conley had jumped in the cab when the shooting started and taken off, still firing back into the action with the rifle he had liked so well. One shot caught Sonny Motley and it was this that stopped his escape more than anything else. In an outburst of violence in the courtroom Sonny shouted that he had shot back at the bastard who double-crossed him and if he didn't hit him, then he'd get him and Torrence someday for sure. They never found the cab, the driver, the money, or Black Conley.

Sonny let me finish and when I handed the papers back said, "It would've gone if Blackie didn't pull out."

"Still sore?"

"Hell no."

"What do you think happened?"

"Tell you what, Mr. Hammer. I got me a guess. That was a double cross somehow, only a triple cross got thrown in. I think old Blackie wound up cab and all at the bottom of the river someplace."

"The money never showed."

"Nope. That went with Blackie too. Everybody lost. I just hope I did shoot the bastard before he died. I don't see how I coulda missed."

"You're still mad, Sonny."

"Naw, not really. Just annoyed about them thirty years he made me take. That Torrence really laid it on, but hell, he had it made. I was a three-timer by then anyway and would have taken life on any conviction. It sure made Torrence though." He pulled his glasses off, looked at the papers once with disgust, rolled them into a ball, and threw them away from him into a refuse carton. "Frig it. What's the sense thinking on them things?"

He looked older and more tired in that moment than when we came in. I said, "Sure, Sonny, sorry we bothered you."

"No trouble at all, Mr. Hammer. Come in for a shine any time."

On the street Velda said, "Pathetic, wasn't he?"

"Aren't they all?"

We waited there a few minutes trying to flag a cab, then walked two blocks before one cut over to our side and squealed to a stop. A blue panel truck almost caught him broadside, but the driver was used to those simple occupational hazards and didn't blink an eye.

I let Velda off at the office with instructions to get what she could from Pat concerning Basil Levitt and Kid Hand and to try to re-establish some old pipelines. If there were new faces showing in town like Jersey Toby said, there was a reason for it. There was a reason for two dead men and a murder attempt on me. There was a reason for an assassination layout with Sue Devon the target and somebody somewhere was going to know the answers.

When Velda got out I gave the cabbie Sim Torrence's Westchester address and sat back to try and think it out. Traffic was light on the ride north and didn't tighten up until we got to the upper end of Manhattan.

Then it was too thick. Just as the cab slowed for a light somebody outside let out a scream and I had time to turn my head, see the nose of a truck almost in the window, and threw myself across the seat as the cab took a tremendous jar that crushed in the side and sent glass and metal fragments ripping above my head. There was one awful moment as the cab tipped, rolled onto its side, and lay there in that almost total silence that follows the second after an accident.

Up front the cabbie moaned softly and I could smell the sharp odor of gasoline. Somebody already had the front door open and arms were reaching in for the driver. I helped lift him, crawled out the opening, and stood there in the crowd brushing myself off. A couple dozen people grouped around the driver, who seemed more shaken than hurt, and for a change a few were telling him they'd be willing to be witnesses. The driver of the truck had cut across and deliberately slammed into the cab like it was intentional or the driver was drunk.

But there wasn't any driver in the truck at all. Somebody said he had jumped out and gone down into a subway kiosk across the street and acted like he was hurt. He was holding his belly and stumbled as he ran. Then I noticed the truck. It was a blue panel job and almost identical to the one which almost nailed the cab when Velda and I first got in it.

Nobody noticed me leave at all. I took the number of the cab and would check back later, but right now there wasn't time enough to get caught up in a traffic accident.

A block down I got another cab and gave him the same address. At the Torrence estate I told the driver to wait, went up, and pushed the bell chime.

Seeing Geraldine King again was as startling as it was the first time. She was in a sweater and skirt combination that set off the titian highlights in her hair, giving a velvet touch to the bright blue of her eyes. There was nothing businesslike about the way she was dressed. It was there only to enhance a lovely body and delight the viewer. I had seen too many strap marks not to know she was skin naked beneath the sweater.

She caught my eyes, let me look a moment longer, and smiled gently. "Stickler for convention?"

"Not me, honey."

"Women should be like pictures . . . nice to look at."

"Not if you haven't got the price to afford to take them home."

"Sometimes you don't have to buy. There are always free gifts."

"Thanks," I grunted. Then I laughed at her. "You sure must be one hell of a political advantage to have around."

"It helps." She held the door open. "Come on in. Mr. Torrence is in the study."

When I went in Sim pushed some papers aside, stood up, and shook hands. "Glad to see you again, Mike. What can I do for you?"

"Some gal you got there."

"What?" He frowned behind his glasses. "Oh . . . oh, yes, indeed. Now . . ."

"I've been checking out your enemies, Mr. Torrence. Those who wanted to kill you."

"Oh?"

"You said you knew of a dozen persons who threatened to kill you. Would Arnold Goodwin be one?"

"The sex offender?"

"Among other things."

"Yes . . . he made threats. Since he was so young I paid no attention to them. Why?"

"Because he's out and is in violation of his parole. He hasn't reported in for some time."

66

"He was quite an emotionally disturbed young man. Do you think . . . ?"

I shrugged. "Those guys can do anything. They'd hurt anybody to get to the primary object of their hate. I haven't followed through on him, but I will."

"Well, the police should be informed immediately. . . ."

"They will be. His parole officer has him listed already. The thing is, he can cut a wide path before they nail him. Meantime, any protection for Sue or yourself should be direct and personal. I'd suggest an armed guard."

"Mr. Hammer . . . we're coming into an election year. If this kind of thing gets out do you know what it means?"

"So take your chances then."

"I'll have to. Nevertheless, it may be sensible to keep somebody here in the house with me. I think Geraldine can arrange for someone."

"You want me to?"

"No, we'll take care of it."

"Okay then. Incidentally, I saw Sonny Motley."

"Sonny Motley?" He tugged at his glasses and pulled them off. "He was given a life sentence."

"Life ends at thirty years in the pen. He's out. You remember him then?"

"I certainly do! It was that case that made me a public figure. You don't think . . ."

"He's an old guy who runs a shoe shop uptown now. No, he's safe enough. You don't play tough when you're over seventy. Those brick walls took too much out of him. It was a pretty interesting case. Neither Blackie Conley or the loot ever showed up, did it?"

"Mike, we covered every avenue possible looking for that money. We alerted every state, every foreign government . . . but whatever happened to Conley or the money has never come to light."

"What do you think happened?" I asked him. Torrence made a vague gesture with his hands. "If he could have gotten out of the country, effected a successful new identity, and didn't try to make too much of a splash so as to attract attention he could have made it. Others have done it on a smaller scale. So might he. That job

67

was well engineered. Whether or not Conley actually planned a double cross or took off when he saw how the fighting was going, we'll never know, but he got away."

"There was the cab."

"He could have killed the driver and dumped the cab somewhere. He was a ruthless man."

"Sonny seemed to think somebody else got to him."

Torrence shook his head, thinking. "I doubt it. There was still the cab and driver, still the money whose serial numbers were recorded. No, I think Conley made a successful escape. If he did, he's probably dead by now. He was eight years older than Sonny, if I remember right. That would put him in his eighties at the end of this time." He looked at me steadily. "Funny you should bring that up."

"Something's come out of the past, buddy. There's trouble. I'm in the middle of it."

"Yes," he nodded, "you are. Now, how can I be of further help?"

"Look back. No matter how slight it might seem, see who wants you badly enough to try to hurt Sue or yourself."

"I will, Mr. Hammer."

"One more thing."

"What's that?"

"Your former wife."

"Yes?"

"How much did you know about her?" I asked him.

Torrence flinched visibly, dropped his eyes to his hands, then brought them back to my face again. "I assume you went to the trouble of looking into her background."

"I heard a few things."

"Then let me say this . . . I was well aware of Sally's history before marrying her. In way of explanation I'll tell you that I loved her. In way of an excuse you might understand, say there's no accounting for taste. We met when she was in trouble. A business relationship developed into friendship that became love. Unfortunately, she maintained her alcoholism and died because of it. Why do you ask?"

"I was thinking of blackmail possibilities."

"Discard them. Everything is a matter of public record. I wouldn't tolerate blackmail."

"Maybe it hasn't been tried yet."

"What does that mean?"

"I don't know," I said. "There are just some interesting possibilities that have developed. You try to stay ahead of them." I got up and put on my hat. "Okay, if I need anything else I'll stop by."

"I'm always available, Mr. Hammer." With a gesture of dismissal he went back to his papers, so I eased out the door and looked for Geraldine King.

She was in a smaller room toward the front, one that had been converted into a small, but efficiently equipped office. Behind a typewriter, with black-rimmed glasses perched on her nose, she looked like a calendar artist's idea of what a secretary should be. Through the knee well in the desk I could see her skirt hiked halfway up her thighs for comfort and the first thing she did when she saw me in the doorway was reach for the hem and tug it down.

I let out a half-silent wolf whistle and grinned. "Man," I said.

She pulled her glasses off and dropped them in front of her. "Distracting, aren't I?"

"Tell me, honey, how the hell does Torrence work with you around?"

Geraldine chuckled and shrugged. "With ease, that's how. I am a fixture, a political associate and nothing more. I can prance around this house in the buff and he'd never notice."

"Want to bet?"

"No, I mean it. Mr. Torrence is dedicated. His political life is all he knows and all he wants. He's been in public service so long that he thinks of nothing else. Any time he is seen with a woman having supper or at some social function is for a political advantage."

"The female votes?"

"Certainly. Women don't mind widowers who seem to still have a family instinct but they do seem to resent confirmed bachelors."

"That's what the men get for giving them the vote. Look, kid, Sim tells me you've been through a few of his political campaigns."

"That's right."

"He ever have any trouble before?"

"Like what?"

"Something from his past coming out to shake him. Any blackmail attempts or threats against his personal life. He says no, but sometimes these things go through the party rather than the individual."

She sat back, frowning, then shook her head. "I think I'd know of anything like that. The organization is well knit and knows the implications of these things and I would have been told, but as far as I know nothing can interfere with his career. He's exceptionally clean. That's why we were so concerned about Sue's running off. Even a thing like that can effect voting. A man who can't run his own house can hardly be expected to run a state."

"You know he's in a position to be hurt now."

"I realize that." She got up, pushed her chair back, and walked toward me with a swaying stride, not conscious at all of the subtle undulations beneath the tight-fitting sweater and skirt. "Do you think Sue will be all right?"

"She's a big girl. She may not look it, but don't be fooled."

"This business . . . about Mr. Torrence killing her mother."

"That's an idea she'll have to get out of her mind."

Geraldine said, "She dreams it. Dreams can be pretty real sometimes. Her very early childhood couldn't have been very nice. I don't think she ever knew who her father was. If she makes open accusations it can damage Mr. Torrence."

"I'll speak to her. She around?"

"There's a summer house on the south side where she practices. She practically lives there."

She was standing in front of me now, concern deep inside those wild blue eyes. I said, "I'll see what I can do."

Geraldine smiled, reached up slowly, and put her arms around my neck. With the same deliberate slowness she pulled herself on her toes, wet her lips with her tongue, and brought my mouth down to hers. It was a soft teasing, tasting kiss, as if she were sampling the juice from a plum before buying the lot. Her mouth was a

70

warm cavern filled with life and promise, then just as slowly she drew away, smiling.

"Thank you," she said.

I grinned at her. "Thank *you*."

"I could hate you easier than I could like you."

"Which is worse?"

"That you'll have to find out for yourself."

"Maybe I will, baby."

At first I didn't think she was there, then I heard the sounds of a cabinet opening and I knocked on the door. Her smile was like the sun breaking open a cloud and she reached for my hand. "Hello, Mike. Gee I'm glad to see you." She looked past me. "Isn't Velda with you?"

"Not this time. Can I come in?"

She made a face at me and stepped aside, then closed the door.

It was a funny little place, apparently done over to her specifications. One wall was all mirror with a dancer's practice bar against it. Opposite was a record player with a shelf of LP's, a shoe rack with all the implements of the trade, a standup microphone attached to a record player, a spinet piano covered with lead sheets of popular music and Broadway hits, with a few stuffed animals keeping them in place.

The rest of the room was a girl-style den with a studio couch, dresser, cabinets, and a small conference table. Cardboard boxes, books, and a few old-fashioned paper files covered the table and it was these she was going through when I found her.

"What're you up to, Sue?"

"Going through my mother's things."

"She's a long time dead. Face it."

"I know. Would you like to see what she looked like?"

"Sure."

There were a few clippings from the trade papers of the time and some framed night-club shots taken by the usual club photographers and they all showed a well-built blonde with a slightly vacuous expression. Whether it was intended or built in I couldn't tell, but she almost typified the beautiful but dumb showgirl. There were four photos, all taken in night spots long since gone. In two of them she was with a party of six. In the other two there were four people, and in those she was with the same man, a lanky dark-haired guy with deep-set eyes who almost seemed like a hell-fire preacher touring the sin spots for material for a sermon.

"She was pretty," I said.

"She was beautiful," Sue said softly. "I can still remember her face."

"These were taken before you were born." I pointed to the dates on the back of the photos.

"I know. But I can remember her. I remember her talking to me. I remember her talking about *him*."

"Come on, kid."

"Her hair swirled as she made a small negative gesture. "I mean it. She hated him."

"Sue . . . they were married."

"I don't care."

I looked at her sharply. "Want me to be blunt?"

She shrugged and bit into her lip.

"Your mother was an alcoholic. Sim tried everything to dry her out. Alcoholics hate that. If she hated him it was because he wanted to help. Get it out of your mind that he killed her."

"She told me the snake killed her."

"Drunks see snakes and elephants and everything else. Don't go getting wrapped up in an obsession."

"She told me to look for a letter. Someday I'll find it."

"You were three years old. How could you remember those things?"

"I just do."

"Okay, you look for it then. Meanwhile, I want you to do something for me."

"What?"

"Don't cause trouble. You stay out of his hair until we clear this thing up. Promise me?"

"Maybe." She was smiling at me.

"What do you want?"

"Kiss me."

I grunted. "I just got done kissing Geraldine King."

"You're nasty, but I don't care." She sidled around the desk and stood there with her hands behind her back. "I'll take seconds," she said.

72

So I kissed her.

"Not like that."

"How?" The damn game was getting out of hand. The big broads I could handle, but how do you get the kids off your back?

Then she showed me how in a moment of sudden violence that was all soft and tender yet filled with some latent fury I couldn't understand. The contact was brief, but it shook me and left her trembling, her eyes darkly languid and her face flushed.

"I hope you like seconds best."

"By far, kid, only don't do it again." I faked a laugh and held her away. "Stay cool, okay?"

"Okay, Mike."

Then I got out of there and back into the taxi where I gave the driver Pat's address.

CHAPTER SIX

The new Inspector was a transfer from another division, a hard apple I had seen around years ago. His name was Spencer Grebb and one of his passionate hatreds was personnel from other fields poking around in his domain, with first cut going to private investigators and police reporters. From the look he gave me, I seemed to have a special place in his book and was target one on his big S list.

Charles Force was a D.A. out for Charlie Force. He was young, talented, on the way up, and nothing was going to deter his ambition. He was a nice-looking guy, but you couldn't tell what was going on behind his face. He had made it the hard way, in the courtrooms, and was a pro at the game right down the line.

Now they both sat at one side of the room with Pat in the middle, looking at me like I was game they were going to let out of the box long enough to get a running start so that hunting me down would be a pleasure.

After the introductions I said, "You check those slugs out, Pat?"

"Both from the same gun that killed Basil Levitt. You mentioned Marv Kania. Could you identify the guy, the guy who pulled the trigger?"

"If he's Kania I could."

"Try this." Pat flipped a four-by-five photo across the desk and I picked it up.

I looked at it and tossed it back. "That's the one."

"Positive?"

"Positive. He's made two passes at me, once in the office building and today with a truck. It rammed a taxi I was in."

Inspector Grebb had a hard, low voice. "This you reported right away."

"Now I'm doing it. At the moment it could have been a simple traffic accident. I ducked out because I had something to do. Now I'm tying it all in."

His smile was a twisted thing. "You know, it wouldn't
74

be too hard to find a charge to press there, would it, Mr. Force?"

Charlie Force smiled too, but pleasantly. A courtroom smile. "I don't think so, Inspector."

As insolently as I could make it, I perched on the edge of Pat's desk and faced them. "Let's get something straight. I know what you guys would like to see, but I'm not going to fall easily. The agency I represent is Federal. It's obscure, but pulls a lot of weight, and if you want to see just how much weight is there, push me a little. I'm operating in an official capacity whether you like it or not, which gives me certain latitudes. I've been around long enough to know the score on both ends so play it straight, friends. I'm cooperating with all departments as Captain Chambers will tell you. Just don't push. You'd be surprised what kind of a stink I can raise if I want to."

I looked at Charlie Force deliberately. "Especially in the publicity circuit, buddy."

His eyebrows pulled together. "Are you threatening me, Mr. Hammer?"

I nodded and grinned at him. "That I am, buster. That's one edge I have on you. A bad schmear and you can go down a notch and never hit the big-time. So play ball."

They didn't like it, but they had to take it. In a way, I couldn't blame them a bit. An ex private jingle coming in with a big ticket isn't easy to take. Especially not one with a reputation like mine.

The D.A. seemed to relax. He was still smiling, but it wasn't for real. "We've been advised to cooperate."

Thanks, Rickerby, I thought. *You're still paying for The Dragon.*

Pat said, "We ran a pretty thorough check on Basil Levitt."

"Anything?"

"We located a girl he used to shack up with. She told us he was on a job but wouldn't say what it was. He said he was getting paid well for it but there would be more later and he was already making big plans. Outside of a few others who knew he had fresh money on him, nothing."

"What about the rifle?"

"Stolen from a sporting goods store upstate about a month ago. We had the numbers on file. He must have worn gloves in the room where he had the gun set up, but got careless when he loaded the clip. There was a single print that tied him in with it."

Before I could answer, Charlie Force said, "Now what we are interested in knowing is who he was shooting at."

I looked at my watch and then at his face. "Art Rickerby clued you in. You know what Velda was involved with."

"Yes," he agreed pleasantly. "We know. But I'm beginning to wonder about it all."

"Well, stop wondering."

"You were there too. Right in the middle."

"Fresh on the scene. Levitt had been there some time. Days."

"Waiting for you?"

Let them think it, I figured. I wasn't cutting him in on anything. "I'm trying to find that out too," I told him. "When I do you'll get the word."

Grebb and Force got up together and headed for the door. Their inspection trip was over. They were satisfied now that I'd make a good target. Grebb looked at me through those cold eyes, still smiling twistedly. "Be sure to do that," he said.

When they were gone Pat shook his head. "You don't make friends easily."

"Who needs them?"

"Someday you will."

"I'll wait until then. Look, buddy, you know what the action is in town?"

Pat just nodded.

"Dickerson?"

He spread his hands. "We're working on it."

"How can a wheel come in already operating and not be known?"

"It isn't hard. You want to know what we have?"

"Damn right."

"Hoods are showing up from all over the country. They're all clean, at least clean enough so we can't tumble them. We can roust them when we want to, but they

76

have nothing we can pin on them."

"How many?"

"Not an army, but let a dozen wrong types hit town at once and it sets a pattern. Something's about to happen."

"They're not holding a convention."

"No, they're getting paid somehow. Either there's loot being laid out or they're operating under orders. There are Syndicate men in and sitting by nice and quietly waiting for the word. All we can do is wait too. In the meantime there's a shake-up in the rackets. Somebody's got the power to pull strings long enough to get action out of the Midwest and the coast. There's a power play going on and a big one. I wish I could figure it out."

He sat there drumming his fingertips on the desk top. "What do *you* think, Mike?"

I gave it to him straight, right down the line, laying the facts face up from the time I walked into the apartment until I reached his office. I watched his mind close around the details and put them into mental cubbyholes to hold there until he had time to assimilate them. But I gave him no opinions, nothing more than facts.

Finally he said, "There are some strange implications."

"Too many."

"I suppose you want something from me now."

"Yeah. Get a killer off my back."

His eyes touched mine and narrowed. "We'll do all we can. He can't get around too long with a bullet in him."

"Up to now he's been doing great."

I got up off the desk and put on my hat. "This Arnold Goodwin . . ."

"I'll get a team out on it. This is one of the implications I don't like. These are the real potential killers. Whether Torrence likes it or not, I'll see that somebody is staked out around his house. We'll keep it quiet, so what he doesn't know won't hurt him."

"Good deal. I'll see you later."

"By the way, Joey Adams called here for you. He wants to see you about something." He grinned at me. "Said he got stopped on a traffic violation and flashed his honorary badge with all the little diamonds and just found out from the arresting officer what it was good for."

"Old joke."

"Funny though."

I called Joey from downstairs and had him meet me in the Blue Ribbon. It was between the meal hours and nobody was there, so George and I sipped coffee until he got there.

After he ordered milk and cake I said, "What's the bit?"

"Look, you had me chasing down Sally Devon's old friends. Well, I'm up in the office when Pauline Coulter comes in to tell me what she forgot. About a week ago she ran into Annette Lee who was with Sally when she died."

"Man, she was old then."

"She's older now, but still kicking. Annette Lee used to be a wardrobe mistress in a show Sally worked in and afterwards worked for Sally as sort of personal maid. Now how about that? You think I'll make a cop yet?"

"Not if you keep flashing that police badge." I grinned.

"Come on!"

"Okay, it was a joke." I laughed. "No kidding though . . . this Lee gal might clean up a few things. It's nice to have friends in important places."

"Anytime, Mike." He pulled out a card and scribbled down an address. "Here's where she is. It's a rooming house across town. She never goes anywhere so you can always find her home."

I stuck the card in my pocket. "How about now? You free?"

"Like a bird, man."

Annette Lee had a front room downstairs in one of the countless brownstones along the street. Her pension money kept her adequately, her cat kept her company, and whatever went on outside her window was enough to keep her busy. She was a small woman, shrunken with age, but in the straight-back rocker, with tiny feet pushing against the floor with tireless rhythm to keep her in motion, she had a funny pixyish quality that was reflected in her faded gray eyes.

There was no telling her accurate age, but it had crept up on her so that her talk wandered into peculiar directions and it was difficult to keep her on one track. But she remembered Sally Devon well. They had been good friends and it was Sally who had taken her in when she was sick and needed an operation, and Sally who cared for her and paid her expenses, so that when Sally needed her, she was glad to go.

She eyed us sharply when I questioned her about Sally's background, but until she was aware that I knew about her past, was reluctant to talk about it. It was Sally's earnings in the seamier side of life that paid her expenses and she was grateful. Little by little she gave it to us. Sally had left show business to take up with men, had gotten involved with the wrong ones and found herself in trouble.

Yes, she knew Sim Torrence, and although she didn't like him, thought he had done well by Sally. He had taken her in when she needed help, and if it hadn't been for Sally's drinking the marriage might have been successful. What she thought was that Sally's guilt complex for bringing a tarnished background into Sim Torrence's life drove her to alcoholism.

She remembered the night Sally died, too. Outside in the cold. Drunk. It was a shame. She couldn't revive her. I asked her directly if she thought Sim Torrence had anything to do with Sally's death.

Annette Lee gave me a shriveling glance. "Don't be silly," she said.

"Just clearing up a point," I told her.

"Then what's this all about, young man?"

"Sue thinks so."

"Sally's little baby?"

"That's right."

"Rubbish. She was only a mite."

"Maybe," I said. "But she's pretty insistent about it. One minute she has the idea Torrence was responsible, the next she says it was a snake."

Annette's face pulled into a tight expression and for a moment her eyes were less faded-looking. "Snake? Sally used to talk about that. When she was drunk. She kept mentioning the snake. Funny you should bring it up. Never thought it would make an impression on a child. Yes, she used to talk about the snake all right. But no snake killed her. She died right there in the front

79

yard, right in my arms. Like to froze, the poor thing did, all drunk up and sick. Maybe it was for the best though."

She sat back in the rocker and closed her eyes. Too much talking was wearing her down. I motioned to Joey and we got up. "Well," I said, "thanks for the talk. Maybe I'll come back again sometime."

"Please do."

We walked to the door as the rhythm of her rocking slowed down. Just as I was about to leave it picked up again and she said, "Young man . . ."

"Ma'am?"

"They ever catch him?"

"Who's that?"

"The one who ran off with all that money. A whole lot of money. Sally's old boy friend."

I called Joey back in and shut the door. "A lot of money?"

"Indeed. Three million dollars. Conley, I think his name was. Blackie Conley. He was a mean one. He was the meanest of them all. They ever catch him?"

"No, they never did."

With her eyes still closed she shook her head. "Never thought they would. He was a thinker. Even heard where he was going after they stole it."

"Where, Miss Lee?" I asked softly.

She didn't answer. She was asleep.

"*Damn*," I said.

The picture was suddenly getting a sharp outline.

I dropped Joey at his AGVA office and went back to my own where Velda was waiting. She had compiled a report on Del Penner for me and from what it looked like he was in solidly now, a natural inheritor of Kid Hand's old territory. It was a step up and he was ready for it, taking advantage of an occupational hazard. Nothing was solidified yet, but he was there and holding on.

When I finished it I got Pat on the phone, asked him if he could pull a package on Blackie Conley from the file, then told Velda to run over and pick it up. When she left I sat back in my chair and swung around so I could stare out the window at the concrete escarpment that was New York.

80

It was getting dark out and a mist was closing in. Another hour and it would be raining again. The multi-color neons of the city were bursting against the gray overcast like summer heat lightning and someplace across town a siren wailed. Another followed it.

Trouble out there. Trouble all over, but trouble out there all the time. Someplace was a guy with a slug in him and a gun in his hand. Someplace was Marv Kania, hurting like hell, waiting for me to show up so he could put one in my gut too. It was Levitt who had done it, but me in his mind. I was the living one, so I did it. Screw him. Let him hurt.

Three million dollars. That could bring trouble to a city. That could bring a man back to power and buy muscle. That was big starter money and a prize for anybody.

Sim Torrence thought Blackie Conley could have made it. Okay, suppose he did. Suppose he sat on that three million all these years, afraid to spend it, not wanting to convert it because of the loss he'd take in the transaction. He just sat on it. It was power to him. Brother, he sure waited for the heat to cool, but it happens like that sometimes. Harmony Brothers sat on a million and a half for forty-one years and only told where it was on his deathbed. Frankie Boyle kept seventy thousand in his mattress for sixteen years, sleeping happily on it every night without ever touching it, then went out of his mind when the rooming house was burned down along with his unspent fortune.

So Blackie Conley got away and sat on three million for thirty years. In the last of his life he gets a power complex and wants to buy his way back in. He'd know how to do it all right. If he could stay under cover thirty years he could still do it.

Blackie Conley! Mr. Dickerson.

A big, fat possible.

Question: *Why try to knock off Sue Devon?*

Answer: A cute possible here too. If Blackie was in love with Sally, and IF Sally had a child by another man, there might be enough hatred to want the child destroyed.

There was only one thing wrong with the premise. Too many people wanted Sue dead. Basil Levitt was

81

trying for it when Kid Hand and Marv Kania came in.

But there was an answer to that one too, a money answer. Sue was a target with a price on her head and if it were big enough the shooters would fight each other for a crack at her. Kid Hand could use the dough and make himself a big one in somebody's eyes at the same time. That could explain why Levitt came in so fast after I got there. He thought I was after head money too.

Blackie Conley, Mr. Dickerson, three million bucks. And the vultures.

Velda came in then and laid the package on my desk. Inside the folder was a picture of Conley. I had seen one like it not too long before in Sue's room. Blackie Conley was the guy in the night clubs with Sally Devon.

His arrest history went back to when he was a child and if he were alive today he'd be eighty-two years old. There were a lot older people still around and some of them right up there with the best. Age doesn't hit everybody the same way.

Pat had included some notes for me suggesting I go into a transcript of the trial if I wanted more information on Conley since it was the last that he was ever mentioned. He was tied in with the gang and his history brought out, but since the trial was a prolonged affair it would take a lot of reading to pick out the pieces.

I looked up at Velda and she stuck her tongue out at me. "I know, you want me to do it."

"You mind?"

"No, but what am I looking for?"

"Background on Conley."

"Why don't you ask Sonny Motley?"

"I intend to, kitten. We have to hit it from all sides."

I filled in the picture for her, watching her face put it together like I did. She nodded finally and said, "You could have it, Mike. It . . . seems right."

"But not quite?"

She ran the tip of her tongue between her teeth. "I just have a feeling."

"I know. Missing pieces. Suppose you meet Annette' Lee and see if you can get any more out of her. It won't come easy, but try. She might give you someplace to start with Conley too."

"Okay, lover."

"And be careful, honey. That nut Kania is still loose. So is Arnold Goodwin. Those guys could be keys to this thing."

"Pat said he'd call you if anything came in on them."

"Good."

"And he said to tell you Charlie Force is protesting your association with the agency you work for."

"He knows what he can do."

"That Inspector Grebb is trouble. He's covering you like a blanket. Do you know you have a tail waiting downstairs?"

"I expected it. I know a way out too."

"You're asking for it, wise guy. I just don't want to see you get killed, that's all. I want to kill you myself. It'll take days and days."

"Knock it off." I swung off my chair and stood up. She grinned, kissed me lightly, and picked up her handbag.

"I arranged for an apartment for you. It's furnished and the key's in the desk. It's got a big double bed."

"It's polite to wait till you're asked."

Velda cocked her head and smiled. "There's a couch in the living room if you still want to be the gentleman."

"Can't you wait until we get married?"

"No." She pulled on her raincoat and belted it. "If I don't push you you'll never come."

"I suppose you have a key."

"Naturally."

"Change the damn lock."

She made a face and walked to the door. "So I'll do like you and shoot it off. *Adios*, doll."

Sonny Motley had closed his shop an hour ago, but the newsboy was still in his kiosk and told me the old guy had a beer or so every night in a joint two blocks down.

It was a sleazy little bar that had sort of just withered within the neighborhood, making enough to keep going, but nothing more. A half-dozen tables lined one wall and the air smelled of beer and greasy hamburgers. Two

83

old broads were yakking it up at the bar, a couple of kids were at the other end watching the fights on TV while they pulled at their drinks, and Sonny Motley sat alone at the last table with a beer in front of him and a late-edition tabloid open in front of him. Beside his feet was a lunchbox and change of a dollar on the table.

I sat down opposite him and said, "Hello, Sonny."

He looked up, closed the paper, and gave me a half-toothless smile. "By damn, didn't expect you. Good you should come. I don't see many people socially."

"This isn't exactly social."

" 'Course not. When does a private cop and a con get social? But for me any talk is social. Sometimes I wish I didn't finish my time. At least then I'd get to see a parole officer for a chat once in a while. But who the hell has time for an old guy like me?"

"Ever see any of your old mob, Sonny?"

"Come on . . . what's your name? Hammer . . ." He ticked off his fingers, "Gleason, Tippy Wells, Harry the Fox, Guido Sunchi . . . all dead. Vinny Pauncho is in the nuthouse up by Beacon and that crazy Willie Fingers is doing his big stretch yet in Atlanta. I wrote to Willie once and never even heard back. Who's left?"

"Blackie Conley."

"Yeah, he's left dead."

"Sim Torrence thinks he might have made it."

"Baloney."

I told the bartender to bring me a beer and turned back to Sonny. "Suppose he did."

"So let him."

"Suppose he came back with the three million bucks you guys heisted?"

Sonny laughed abruptly and smacked his hands on the table. "That would be the funniest yet. What the hell could he do with it? All that stud wanted was broads and at his age it would be like shoving a wet noodle up a tiger's . . . no, Hammer, it wouldn't do him no good at all." He sat back and chuckled at the thought and waved for another beer.

"Let's consider it," I insisted.

"Sure, go ahead."

"So he's old. He wants one more crack at the big-time."

"Who the hell would listen to him?"

"You could pull a power play from behind the scenes. Three million bucks can do a lot of talking and if somebody is fronting for you who knows what you look like?"

Sonny stopped smiling then, his face wrapped in thought. Then he dragged on the beer and put half of it down at once. "No," he said, "Blackie ain't coming back, Hammer. He never ain't."

"Why not?"

His grin was tight-lipped, satisfied with what he was thinking. "Because I nailed old Blackie, I did. Man, with a rod I was good. I mean good, Hammer. You know he got me with that damn rifle. It put me down and stopped me, but I had one chance at him when he took off in that taxi and let one go while he still had the rifle poked out the window. I didn't miss with that shot. I think I got old Blackie and he crawled off and died or wound himself and the taxi both up in the drink."

"Maybe."

"Okay, so I'm wrong. Hope I am." He chuckled again and finished the beer. "Like to see old Blackie again. I'd like to find out if I really did get him or not."

"Ever hear of Mr. Dickerson?" I asked him.

"Nope. Should I?"

"Not especially."

"Who is he?"

"I don't know either."

"Like hell you don't."

"Why do you say that?" I asked him.

"Because I've lived with cons too damn long, Hammer. You get so you can tell things without them having to be said. Take now, f'instance. You ain't asked all you came here to ask yet, have you?"

It was my turn to buy and I yelled for another brew. "Okay, old-timer, I'll put it straight. You remember Sally Devon?"

Sonny frowned slightly and wiped his mouth with the back of his hand. "Sure. Used to be my broad."

"I thought she was Conley's."

"That bastard would go after anything in skirts no matter who she belonged to."

"Even yours?"

"Sure. I warned him off a few times. Had to knock

85

him on his kiester once. But hell, what difference does it make? In those days he was a sharp article. Older than we were and pretty smooth. Sally was always sweet on him. If I didn't bounce her around she woulda left me for him any day."

He stopped suddenly, his eyes going cold. "You're thinking maybe because of her Blackie dumped the heist and tried to take me?"

"Could be."

Then the coldness left his eyes and the age came back. He let out a muted cackle and shook his head at the joke. "Damn," he said, "that guy was always thinking."

"Where were you going with the money if that job paid off, Sonny?"

"What's the matter, don't you read?"

"You tell me."

He bobbed his head, relishing the moment. "I even see it done on some TV shows now, but it woulda worked. We had a truck with a tailgate ramped down. We was to drive the cab right in there and take off. So the cops found the truck and another one we was going to change to. It's all down. Instead that Bastard Blackie crossed us."

"What were you going to do to the driver?"

"Toss him out, bump him. Who knows? We woulda figured somethin'."

"You had a hideout?"

"Yeah, a house in the Catskills we had rented ahead of time. The cops plastered that looking for Blackie. He made all the arrangements on that end and never got to use 'em. Coulda been the crime of the century."

"Maybe it was," I said.

Sonny was reaching for his glass and stopped short. "What're you thinking, boy?"

"Maybe while Blackie was making plans for you he was making other plans for himself. Suppose he arranged for an alternate hideout and made it after all. Suppose he bumped the driver, ditched the car, and holed up all these years and finally decided to come back again. Now he's here with three million bucks taking his last fling, buying himself an organization."

He listened, sat silent a moment, then shook his head and picked up his beer. "Not old Blackie. He couldn't live without the broads and now he's too old."

"Ever hear of a voyeur?"

"What's that?"

"They can't do it so they just watch. I know a few old jokers who get their kicks that way. They got millions too."

"I think you're nuts," he said, "but any time you want to talk about it come back and talk. You're the first company I had around in a long time."

"Sure." I wrote down my new address on a matchbook cover and passed it to him. "Reach me here or at the office if you get any ideas. You can earn some cash."

I put a buck on the table and left. Behind me Sonny was still chuckling. I'd like to be there if he ever got to meet Blackie face to face.

CHAPTER SEVEN

I called Hy from a drugstore on the avenue and got
Pete Ladero's address from him. I reached him at
home and asked him if he could get the newspaper clips
on the Motley-Conley job thirty years ago and bring
them up to the office. He griped about leaving his favorite
TV program, but his nose for news was too big and
he said it would take an hour, but he'd be there.

At the Automat on Sixth between Forty-fourth and
Forty-fifth I picked up a tray, loaded it with goodies,
and went upstairs to think for a while. It wasn't accidental.
I knew Jersey Toby would be there the same as he
had been there at the same time every night the past
ten years. I let him finish his meal, picked up my coffee,
and joined him at his table. When he saw me he almost
choked, gave a quick look around, and tightened up.

"Damn, can't you get off my neck? Whatta you want?"

"Talk, Toby, just talk."

"Well, I said all I'm gonna say. Scratch off, Mike.
I don't want no part of you, buddy. You know I got
asked questions already?"

"Who asked?"

"Some broad in the other joint. She knew you all
right. I tried to lie out of it and said you was looking
for a dame for that night but she wouldn't buy it. Said
she knew you too well. You're hooked for somebody
else. You're putting my tail in a sling."

"So I'll make it short."

"Like hell. You won't make nothing."

"Okay, Toby, then tomorrow a pickup goes out
on you. You get rousted every time you step on the
street. Lineup twice a week, complaints . . ."

Jersey Toby looked at me, his face white and drawn.
"Come on, you wouldn't do that."

"Try me."

He finished his coffee, looked around nervously again
until he was assured we were alone, and nodded. "You
would at that. Okay, spill it."

"Let's go back to Dickerson again, Toby."

"We went through that once."

"You get the word."

"Sure . . . secondhand through the broads."

"Good enough. What's the word on the money angle? If out-of-town hoods are moving in, something's drawing them. Who's spreading the green around?"

Toby's tongue flicked at dry lips and he pulled on the butt. "Look . . . if I prime you, this is the last?"

I shrugged.

"Let's hear it, Mike."

"You bought it. I'll back off."

"Okay then, Marge . . . she's the redhead. She was with . . . a guy one night. No names, Mike. I ain't giving you names. I specialize in that end of the trade. Marge, she's a favorite with the hard boys. Does a lot of fancy tricks for them, see? Well, this guy . . . like he's representing somebody big. He's like muscle on lend. He comes in to do a favor. He's Chicago and ready. He ain't saying what's to do, but he stands ready. Now his boss man lends him out because a favor was asked, only his boss man don't *do* no favors. It's got to be bought or got to be forced. Somebody's got something on his boss man and is making a trade.

"Don't ask what it is. Who am I to know? I just put two and two together until it works out. Somebody is building an organization and although money is there it's the pressure that's bringing the boys in."

I tipped back in the chair watching him. "It plays if somebody is building an organization. Whatever the pressure is, it brings muscle in that can't be bought, then the muscle can be used to square the money."

"You play it," Toby said. "I don't even want to think on it no more."

"How many are in?"

"Enough. With a mob like's here I could damn near run the town single-handed."

"These boys all come from big sources?"

Toby's head bobbed once. "The biggest. The Syndicate's lending men. They come out of the individual operations, but the boss men are the Syndicate men. You're trouble, boy."

"Thanks, kiddo. You've been a help."

"For that I ain't happy. I hope they get you before they tie me into anything."

"Forget it," I said and got up from the table.

I left him there and walked out into the rain back toward my office. If Jersey Toby was right Mr. Dickerson was pulling off a cute trick. It figured right, too, because he'd be smart enough and would have had the time to work it out. Little by little he could have built the things he needed to pressure the big ones into line. He had the background, experience, and the desire. One thing led to another. Once the mob was in, an organization could be built that could utilize three million bucks properly.

If Mr. Dickerson was Blackie Conley it fitted just right.

Up in the office I had to wait only fifteen minutes before Pete Ladero came in with a folio under his arm. He laid the stuff on the table and opened it up. "Do I get an explanation first?"

"Research on Blackie Conley," I said.

"Aw, for crying out loud, he's been dead for years."

"Has he?"

"Well . . ." He paused and searched my face. "You on to something?"

"You familiar with this case?"

"I ran over it. The magazine writers rehashed it enough so I know the general background. Give."

"If Conley's alive he's got three million bucks in his kick. He might be old and fiesty enough to start trouble with it."

"Boy, bring-'em-back-alive Hammer." He reached for the paper. "You looking for anything special?"

"Conley's connection with the heist. Take half and we'll go through them."

So we sat down and read. Velda called and I told her to hop over, then went back to the papers again.

The prosecution had a cut-and-dried case. Sonny Motley pleaded guilty since he was nailed in the act and faced an automatic sentence anyway. He ranted and raved all the way through the trial, cursing everybody from the judge down, but Torrence and Conley in particular. Torrence because he wouldn't let him alone, but kept hammering for details, and Conley for the big double-cross and a bullet in his shoulder.

The main item of interest was the missing three million dollars, but despite the speculation and the nationwide police search, not one thing was turning up. Sonny Motley didn't mind spilling his guts if it meant nailing Blackie Conley and the unseen face who engineered the deal. Right then he figured they pulled the double-cross together, but Sim Torrence couldn't get any evidence whatsoever on the one behind the action.

There was another witness. Her name was Sally Devon and she was called because she was assumed to be a confederate of Sonny's. Her testimony was such that she turned out to be the beautiful but dumb type after all, knowing nothing of the mob's operation. Sonny and the others all admitted she was only a shack job as far as they were concerned and that seemed to end her part in the affair. Only one reporter mentioned a statement that had any significance. Just before she was discharged from the stand she said that *"she'd like to get the snake that was responsible."*

And that was what had bothered me. Sue had said the same thing, only there had been a minor discrepancy in her statements. First she said it was *a* snake that had killed her mother. Later she said *the* snake! Sue Devon remembered something, all right. Sally had raved in her drunkenness too . . . not about snakes . . . but about *the* snake. Old Mrs. Lee just hadn't understood right.

Now The Snake was emerging. It was the one who engineered the whole damn business. The one nobody knew about or saw. The one who could have engineered it into a massive double-cross to start with.

Blackie Conley. He really played it cute. He stood by as a lieutenant to Sonny Motley, but it was his plan to start with. He worked it into a cross and took off with the profits. He was bigger than anybody gave him credit for being. He was big enough to hold on until he felt like it and make the most incredible comeback in the history of crime.

If it worked.

And it was working.

I had been looking over the paper too long. Pete said, "You found it, didn't you?"

"I think I have."

"Do I get it?"

"Why not?" I put the paper down and looked at him. "Can you hold it?"

"Better tell me about it first."

When I did he whistled softly and started writing. I said, "If it goes out now this guy might withdraw and we'll never get him. You can call the shots, buddy, but I'd advise you to wait. It could be bigger."

He put the pencil away, grinning. "This is bonus stuff, Mike. I'll sit on it. Make it mine though, will you?"

"Done."

"Want Hy in?"

"Damn right. The office can use the publicity. Give him the same poop."

"Sure, Mike." He folded the news clips together and headed for the door. "Call me when you need anything."

I waved when he left, then picked up the phone and dialed Pat. He was home for a change, and sore about being dragged out of bed. I said, "How'd you make out, Pat?"

"Got something new for you."

"Oh?"

"Write off Arnold Goodwin. He's dead."

"What happened?"

"He was killed a couple of months ago in an automobile accident near Saratoga. His body's been lying in a morgue up there unclaimed. The report just came in with his prints."

"Positive?"

"Look, it was a stiff with good prints. He was on file. He checked out. The dead man was Goodwin. The accident involved a local car and was just that . . . an accident."

"Then it narrows things down. You still working on Basil Levitt?"

"All the way. We've gone over his record in detail and are trying to backtrack him up to the minute he died. It won't be easy. That guy knew how to cover a trail. Two of my men are working from a point they picked up three months ago and might be able to run it through. Incidentally, I have an interesting item in his history."

"What's that?"

"After he lost his P.I. license he had an arrest record of nineteen. Only two convictions, but some of the charges were pretty serious. He was lucky enough each time to have a good lawyer. The eleventh time he was picked up for assault and it was Sim Torrence who defended him and got him off."

"I don't like it, Pat."

"Don't worry about it. Sim was in civil practice at the time and it was one of hundreds he handled. Levitt never used the same lawyer twice, but the ones he used were good ones. Torrence had a damn good record and the chances are the tie-in was accidental. We got on this thing this morning and I called Torrence personally. He sent Geraldine King up here with the complete file on the case. It meant an hour in court to him, that's all, and the fee was five hundred bucks."

"Who made the complaint?"

"Some monkey who owned a gin mill but who had a record himself. It boils down to a street fight, but Torrence was able to prove that Levitt was merely defending himself. Here's another cute kick. Our present D.A., Charlie Force, defended Levitt on charge seventeen. Same complaint and he got him off too."

"Just funny that those two ever met."

"Mike, in the crime business they get to meet criminals. He does, I do, and you do. Now there's one other thing. The team I have out are circulating pictures of Levitt. Tonight I get a call from somebody who evidently saw the photo and wanted to know what it was all about. He wouldn't give him name and there wasn't time to get a tracer on the call. I didn't tell him anything but said that if he had any pertinent information on Levitt to bring it to us. I was stalling, trying for a tracer. I think he got wise. He said sure, then hung up. As far as we got was that the call came from Flatbush."

"Hell, Pat, that's where Levitt comes from."

"So do a couple million other people. We'll wait it out. All I knew was that it was an open phone, not a booth unless the door was left open, and probably

93

in a bar. I could hear general background talk and a juke going."

"We'll wait that one out then. He has something on his mind."

"They usually call again," Pat said. "You have anything special?"

"Some ideas."

"When do I hear them?"

"Maybe tomorrow."

"I'll stand by."

When I hung up I stared at the phone, then leaned my face into my hands trying to make the ends meet in my mind. Screwy, that's all I could think of. Screwy, but it was making sense.

The phone rang once, jarring me out of my thought. I picked it up, said hello, and the voice that answered was tense. "Geraldine King, Mike. Can you come out here right away?"

"What's up, Geraldine?"

She was too agitated to try to talk. She simply said, "Please, Mike, come right away. *Now*. It's very important." Then she gave me no choice. She hung up.

I wrote a note to Velda telling where I was going and that I'd head right back for the apartment when I was done, then left it in the middle of her desk.

Downstairs I cut around back of the cop assigned to watch me, took the side way out without being seen, and picked up a cruising cab at the street corner. The rain was heavier now, a steady, straight-down New York rain that always seemed to come in with the trouble. Heading north on the West Side Highway I leaned back into the cushions and tried to grab a nap. Sleep was out of the question, even for a little while, so I just sat there and remembered back to those last seven years when forgetting was such a simple thing to do.

All you needed was a bottle.

The cop on the beat outside Torrence's house checked my identity before letting me go through. Two reporters were already there talking to a plainclothesman and a fire captain, but not seeming to be getting much out of either one of them.

Geraldine King met me at the door, her face tight and worried.

I said, "What happened?"

"Sue's place . . . it burned."

"What about the kid?"

"She's all right. I have her upstairs in bed. Come on inside."

"No, let's see that building first."

She pulled a sweater on and closed the door behind us. Floodlights on the grounds illuminated the area, the rain slanting through it obliquely.

There wasn't much left, just charred ruins and the concrete foundation. Fire hoses and the rain had squelched every trace of smoldering except for one tendril of smoke that drifted out of one corner, and I could see the remains of the record player and the lone finger that was her microphone stand. Scattered across the floor were tiny bits of light bouncing back from the shattered mirror that had lined the one wall. But there was nothing else. Whatever had been there was gone now.

I said, "We can go back now."

When we were inside Geraldine made us both a drink and stood in the den looking out the window. I let her wait until she was ready to talk, finishing half my drink on the way. Finally she said, "This morning Sue came inside. I . . . don't know what started it, but she came out openly and accused Mr. Torrence of having killed her mother. She kept saying her mother told her."

"How could she say her mother told her she was murdered when she was alive to tell her?" I interrupted.

"I know, I know, but she insisted her mother wrote something and she was going to find it. You know she kept all her mother's old personal things out there."

"Yes, I saw some of them."

"Mr. Torrence is in the middle of an important campaign. He was quite angry and wanted this thing settled once and for all, so while Sue was in here he went out and went through her things, trying to prove that there was nothing.

"Sue must have seen him from upstairs. She came down crying, ran outside, and told him to leave. Neither one of us could quiet her down. She locked herself inside and wouldn't come out and as long as she was there we didn't worry about it. This . . . wasn't exactly the first time this has happened. We were both used to her outbursts.

"Late this afternoon Mr. Torrence got a call and had to leave for his office on some campaign matter. It was about two hours later that I happened to look out and saw the smoke. The building was burning from the inside and Sue was still there. The record player was going and when I looked in the window she was doing some crazy kind of dance with one of those big stuffed toys that used to belong to her mother.

"She wouldn't come out, wouldn't answer me . . . nothing. I . . . guess I started screaming. There was a policeman outside the fence, fortunately. He just happened to be there."

I shook my head. "No, he wasn't. This department was cooperating with the requests of the city police. He was there purposely. Go on."

"He came in and broke down the door. By that time Sue was almost unconscious, lying there on the floor with the flames shooting up the walls. We dragged her out, got her in the house, and I put her to bed. One of the neighbors saw the flames and called the fire department. They came, but there was nothing to do. The damage was not really important . . . except now we'll never know what Sue had of her mother's that she was always searching for."

"Where was Torrence at this time?"

Slowly, she turned around, fingering the drink in her hand. "I know what you're thinking, but perhaps twenty minutes before that I spoke to him on the phone. He was in the city."

"How can you be sure?"

"Because I spoke to two others in his office on some party matters."

"Where is he now?"

"On the way to Albany with some of his constituents. If you want I'll see that he's notified and we'll get him right back."

"I don't think it's necessary. Can I see Sue?"

"She'll be asleep. She was totally worn out. She started the fire, you know."

"I don't."

"But I do."

96

"How?"

"She told me. She'll tell you too when she's awake."

"Then we'll awaken her."

"All right."

Sue's bedroom was a composite of little girl and grown-up. There were framed still pictures of Sally Devon on her dresser and vanity along with some of herself in leotards and ballet costumes. There was another record player here and an almost identical stack of classical L.P.'s. Scattered here and there were toys from another year, mostly fuzzy animals and dolls in dancing clothes.

She lay in bed like a child, her yellow hair spilling around her face, one arm snuggling an oversized animal whose fur had been partially burned off, the face charred so that it was almost unrecognizable for whatever it was. She smiled dreamily, held the toy close to her, and buried her face against it. Some of the straw was sticking out on one side and she pushed it out of the way.

I touched her arm. "Sue . . ."

She didn't awaken immediately. I spoke her name twice again before she opened her eyes.

She said, "Hello, Mike."

"Sue . . . did you set the fire?"

"Yes, I was . . . burning Mother's old papers. I didn't want him to see anything of hers."

"What happened?"

She smiled again. "I . . . don't know. Everything . . . seemed to start burning. I sort of felt happy then. I didn't care. I sang and danced while it was burning and felt good. That's all I remember."

"Okay, go back to sleep."

"Mike . . ."

"What?"

"I'm sorry."

"That's all right."

"He'll . . . put me away or something now, won't he?"

"I don't think so. It *was* an accident."

"Not really it wasn't. I meant it."

I sat on the edge of the bed and took her hand. She was still in a state of semi-shock and sometimes that's the time when they can say the right thing. I said, "Sue

97

. . . you remember telling me your mother was killed by the snake?"

Her eyes drifted away momentarily, then came back to mine. "The snake did it. She said so. The snake would kill her because he had to."

"Who is the snake, honey?"

"She said the snake would kill her," she repeated "I remember." Her eyes started to widen and under my hand her arm grew taut. "She said . . ."

But I wouldn't let her talk any more. She was too near the breaking point, so I leaned over and kissed her and the fear left her face as suddenly as it appeared and she smiled.

"Go back to sleep, honey. I'll see you in the morning."

"Don't leave, Mike."

"I'll be around."

"Please, Mike."

I winked and stood up. "Sleep, baby, for me."

"All right, Mike."

I left a night light on and the door partly open and went back downstairs with Geraldine. I sat back on the couch and took the drink she made me, sipping i slowly.

Outside the rain slapped at the windows, massaging them with streaky, wet fingers. She turned on the record player, drew the heavy draperies across the windows and turned out all the lights except one. Then she sa down beside me.

Only then did she say, "What shall we do, Mike?"

"Nothing yet."

"There were reporters out there."

"What did you tell them?"

"That it was accidental. It really wasn't too important . . . just a small outbuilding. If it weren't Mr. Torrence's place it would never draw a mention, but . . . well, you understand."

"They won't make much out of it."

"But if Sue keeps making these accusations . . . it's an election year, Mike. The campaign for governor of a state is of maximum importance. You know how both parties look at it. This is a key state. From here a governor can go into the White House or at least have a major effect on national policy. If anything . . . anything at
98

ll comes up that can be detrimental to a selected candidate can be disastrous. This . . . this business with Sue s getting out of hand."

"Your bunch knows about it then?"

She nodded, then took a swallow of her drink. "Yes . . in a way it's why I'm here. I've been with Sim Torrence on his other campaigns as much as a guardian or Sue as an assistant to Mr. Torrence. She doesn't realize all this and I've made it a point to keep it almost businesslike, but I do manage to find things for Sue to do and distract this antagonistic attitude she has. All her life she's been trying to emulate her mother . . . trying to be a showgirl. She's been coached in singing, dancing, the arts . . . given the very best Mr. Torrence can give her. She's taken advantage of those opportunities, not just to help her into show business but it gets her away from him. Sad, but true."

"You speculating now?"

She looked at me over her glass. "No, she's told me that. You can ask her."

"I believe it."

"What can we do? It's critical now."

"I'll think of something."

"Will you, Mike? We need help badly."

"You sure love this political crap, don't you?"

"My life, Mike. I gave my life to it."

"Hell, you're too young to die. Maybe you should have been born a man."

"There's a place for women in politics."

"Bull."

"You just like them to be women, don't you?"

"That's what they are."

"All right. For you I'll be a woman."

She put her drink down on the coffee table, took mine from my hand and put it next to hers, both unfinished. There was a sudden hunger in her eyes and a warmth to her face that made her mouth seem to blossom into a new fullness. Her fingers went to her throat and one by one she unbuttoned her blouse until it lay open, then with the slightest shrug of her shoulders it slid away so that her fingers could work more magic with the soft fabric of the bra. She whisked it away and it floated to the floor where it lay unnoticed.

I looked at her, not touching her, taking in the lovely slope of her breasts that were swelled with emotion and tipped with the firm pinkness of passion. I could smell the fragrant heat of her only inches away, and as I watched, her stomach undulated and moved spasmodically against the waistband of her skirt.

"How am I . . . as a woman, Mike?"

"Lovely," I told her. I reached for her, turned her around, then lay her as she was, half naked, across my lap, my fingers caught in her hair, touching her gently at first, then with firm insistence that made her shudder.

She raised herself against me, twisting her head, searching for my mouth until she found it, then with a small whimper she was part of me, her lips a ripe, succulent fruit, her tongue an alive, vital organ that was a soul seeking another soul. I let her fall away from me reluctantly, her mouth still working as though it were kissing mine yet, her eyes closed, her breath coming heavily.

Someplace in the house a clock chimed and a dull rumble of thunder outside echoed it. I let my hand run down the naked expanse of her stomach until the tips of my fingers traced a path across her waist under the skirt. She moaned softly and sucked in her breath so there would be a looseness at her belt. I felt her briefly, kneaded the pliant flesh, then took my hand away.

Her eyes opened, she smiled once and closed them again. Then she was asleep. It had been a hard day for her too. I held her until I was sure she wouldn't awaken, then raised her, propped a cushion beneath her shoulders, and let her down onto it. I covered her with her blouse and a plaid car blanket that was folded over the back of a chair.

In the morning she'd feel better. She'd hate me maybe, but then again, maybe not. I went upstairs and checked Sue. She had turned on her side and the oversized stuffed toy was almost crushed beneath her.

I called a cab in from town, let myself out, and waited by the gate. The cop on the beat asked me if everything was all right and I told him the women were both asleep and to stay on his toes. He still couldn't read me but with the card I carried he wasn't taking any chances. He saluted cordially and walked off into the darkness.

Inspector Grebb should have seen that, I thought.

He'd flip. He'd sooner I got a boot in the tail.

When the cab came he didn't want to take me clean into the city so I changed cabs at the George Washington Bridge and gave that driver the address of my new apartment. I started to grin, thinking of what Velda would do if she knew where I was an hour ago. Hell, she never would believe me if I told her the truth anyway, so why say a word? But you can't go through two of those deals in one night and stand up to it. If Velda were there I hoped she was sacked out tight. Right then I needed sleep more than anything I could think of.

I paid the cab off and went inside. The place was freshly renovated and smelled of paint. I took the automatic elevator to the third floor, found my new apartment at the very end of the hall, and stuck the key in the lock. There was a soft glow from a table lamp at the end of the couch in the living room and a radio was playing softly. From where I stood I could see her stretched out comfortable and laughed to myself. Velda had determination, but sleep had won out. She got the couch and I got the bed this time. Tomorrow she'd sizzle, but she'd still be waiting.

I went in on the balls of my feet, walking quietly so as not to waken her, but I couldn't help looking at her as I passed. And when I saw her I turned ice cold inside because she wasn't just asleep at all. Somebody had brought something down across her temple turning it into a livid welt that oozed dark blood under her ear into her hairline.

I grabbed her, said *"Velda!"* once, then she let out a little meowing sound and her eyes flicked open. She tried to talk but couldn't and it was her eyes that got the message across. I looked up to the side where he stood with one hand holding his belly and the other a gun and he had it pointed right at my head.

Marv Kania had finally found me.

His eyes had death in them, his and mine. His belly was bloated and I could smell the stench of a festering wound, the sickening odor of old blood impregnated into cloth. There was a wildness in his face and his mouth was a tight slash that showed all his teeth. Marv Kania was young, but right there he was as old as death itself.

"I was waiting for you, mister."

Slowly, I got up. I was going to have to pull against

101

a drawn gun and there wasn't a chance I could make it. He was dying, but the gun in his hand was there with the deft skill of the professional and it never wavered an inch. He let the muzzle drift down from my head until it pointed at my stomach.

"Right where I got it, man, and there's no coming back after that. Everything inside goes. You'll live a little while and you'll hurt like I hurt. You try to move away from it and I put one more in your head."

I was thinking fast, wondering how fast I could move away from the shot. He knew what I was going to do and grinned through the pain he felt. Just to let me know it was no good he made two quick wrist motions to show he still had it and I had it, then he thumbed the hammer back.

"The girl. What about her?"

"What do you care? You'll be dead."

"What about her?"

His face was a mask of pain and hate. "I'll tell you what I'm going to do. With her she gets one shot. Same as you. Then I go outside and die. Out in the rain, just so long as I don't die in no crummy room. In the park, that's where I die. I always wanted to die there." His eyes half shut momentarily as a spasm of pain took him, then he snapped them open and grinned, his teeth bare against his gums.

Velda turned on the couch, whispering my name softly. She must have come in when he was there. He held a gun on her, belted her out, and kept on waiting. Now he was going to kill her along with me.

"You ready, you bastard?"

I didn't move. I just stood there hoping Velda could do something while my own body half shielded her from him, hoping she could move fast enough to get the hell out. He saw that too and started to laugh. It was so funny to him with all the hate bottled up inside he laughed even harder as he aimed the rod with every ounce of professional technique he ever had.

And it was the laugh that did it. The laugh that broke the last thing inside. The laugh that burst the lifeline. He felt it go and his eyes went so wide the whites of them showed the horror he felt because he was still a loser and before he could put that final fraction of

102

pressure on the trigger the gun dropped from his hand and he pitched face down on the floor with a sickening squashing sound as some ghastly, putrescent fluid burst from his belly.

I picked Velda up, carried her into the bedroom, and washed the blood from her temple. Then I loosened her clothes and pulled the blanket over her before flopping down on the bed beside her.

Outside I had another dead man at my feet, but he was going to have to wait until morning.

CHAPTER EIGHT

Pat was there at nine in the morning. So was Inspector Grebb and Charles Force. Pat's face told me he had no choice so I threw him a brief nod so he knew I got the picture.

The police photographers got all the shots they wanted, the body was carried out, Velda had a doctor in with her, and Grebb pointed at a chair for me and sat down himself.

"You've been a thorn in our side, Hammer," he said pleasantly.

"Tough."

"But I think we have you nailed now."

"For failing to report a body?"

"It's enough. You don't step that far outside and still get a gun-carrying privilege. It will break you with that fancy agency because they like closed mouths about their operations. They lift your ticket and you're back in the ranks again."

Charlie Force was standing there with that same old courtroom smile, like his bait had caught the fish. I said, "I warned you, Charlie."

"Mr. Force, if you don't mind?"

This time I let him see the kind of grin I had, the one with teeth in it. I said, "Okay, buddy, I'll come to your party, only I'm bringing my friends. I'm bringing in pressures you never heard of. Get something in your goddamn heads . . . you're two public servants and all you're looking for is another step up. If you got the idea you'll get it over me you're wrong. Don't think that agency is going to back down a bit. I gave them too much and they're still paying off for it. I'll keep giving them more and more until they can't afford to lose me. The agency is bigger than both you guys and now you're going to find it out the hard way.

"As for you, Force, before you were playing in courtrooms I was pushing a legal gun around this town and there are guys I know and friends I made who'd like nothing better than to wipe your nose in a mess.

Believe me, buddy, if you ever did one lousy thing in your life . . . and you can bet your ass you did because everybody does, I'll nail it down and you'll go with it. It won't even be a hard job. But I'll do even better than that to you, kid. I'll pull the stool right out from under you. This little bugger I'm on now is a hot little bugger and it's mine. You get no slice of it at all. I'll make the action and get the yaks."

I spun around and looked at Pat. "Tell them, friend."

"You did a pretty good job. I'm still a Captain."

"Well, maybe we'll get you raised one after this, okay, Inspector?"

He didn't say anything. He sat there glowering at me, not knowing what to think. But he was an old hand and knew when the wind was blowing bad. It showed in his eyes, only he didn't want me to to see it. Finally he looked at his watch, then up to me. "We'll wait some more," he said. "It's bound to happen sometime."

"Don't hold your breath waiting," I said.

"You take care of things here, Captain," he said to Pat. "I'll want to see the report later."

"I'll have it on your desk, Inspector."

They left then, two quiet men with one idea in their minds nobody was ever going to shake loose. When they were out I said to Pat, "Why the heat?"

"Because the city is on edge, Mike. They haven't got the answers and neither have I. Somehow you always get thrown in the middle of things so that you're the one to pull the switch."

"You got everything I know."

Pat nodded sagely. "Great. Facts are one thing, but there's still that crazy mind of yours. You make the same facts come out different answers somehow." He held up his hand to shut me up. "Oh, I agree, you're cooperative and all that jazz. You lay it on the line like you're requested to do and still make it look like your own idea. But all the time you're following a strange line of reasoning nobody who looks at the facts would take. I always said you should have been a straight cop in the first place."

"I tried it a long time ago and it didn't work."

"You would have made a perfect crook. Sometimes

I wonder just what the hell you really are inside. You live in a half world of your own, never in, never out, always on the edge."

"Nuts to you, Pat. It works."

"The hard way."

Pat walked to the window, stared down into the courtyard a moment, then came back. "Kania say anything to you before he died?"

"Only how he was going to enjoy killing me."

"You didn't ask him any questions?"

"With a gun on me and him ready to shoot? There wasn't anything to ask."

"There wasn't any chance you could have taken him?"

"Not a one."

"So I'll buy it. Now, how'd he find you?"

"I'm not that hard to find. He did it twice before. He probably picked up Velda at my office and followed her here."

"She talk yet?"

"No," I told him, "but maybe she will now. Let's ask her."

The doctor had finished with Velda, assuring us both that it was only a minor concussion that should leave no after-effects, gave me a prescription for a sedative, and left us alone with her.

She smiled up at me crookedly, her face hurting with the effort.

"Think you can talk, kitten?"

"I'm all right."

"How'd that punk get in here?"

She shook her head and winced. "I don't know. I left the door unlocked thinking you'd be in shortly, then I went to the bathroom. When I went back into the living room he stepped out of the bedroom. He held the gun on me . . . then made me lie on the couch. I knew he was afraid I'd scream or something so he just swung the gun at me. I remember . . . coming awake once, then he hit me again. That's all I remember until you spoke to me."

I glanced at Pat. "That's how he did it then. He waited at the office."

"Did you know Grebb kept a man staked out there?"

"Didn't everybody? I told you to stay off my neck."

"It wasn't my idea."

"Kania must have spotted him the same as I did. He simply waited outside or across the street until Velda came out. When she came alone he figured she could lead him to me and stayed with her. She made the job easy by leaving the door open."

"I'm sorry, Mike."

"No sweat, baby," I said. "It won't happen again."

"Mike . . ."

"What?"

"Mrs. Lee. She'd like to see you again."

She was bypassing Pat, but he caught it and grinned. "I haven't heard about her."

"An old lady. Sally Devon's old wardrobe mistress. She was with her when she died. She'll talk to anybody for company's sake but she might come up with something."

"Still going back thirty years?"

"Does money get old?" I asked him.

There was a jack next to the bed so I got the phone from the living room and plugged it in and laid it on the nightstand where Velda could reach it. "You stay put all day, honey. I'll check in with you every now and then and if you want anything, just call down for it. I'll leave your key with the super and he can check on anybody who comes in."

"Mike . . . I'll be fine. You don't have to . . ."

I cut her off. "Look, if I want you for anything, I'll call. There's a lot you can do without getting out of bed. Relax until I need you. Shall I get somebody to stay with you?"

"No."

"I'll be moving fast. I don't know where I'll be. But I'll check in every couple of hours. Maybe Pat here can give you a buzz too."

"Be glad to," he said. There was restraint in his voice and I knew how he was hurting. It isn't easy for a guy who loves a woman to see her going down the road with somebody else. War, love . . . somebody's got to be the loser.

So I covered her up and went outside with Pat. About twenty minutes later two men from his division came in, got a rundown on Kania, and started backtracking

107

him. A contract killer wasn't notorious for leaving a trail, but Marv Kania had a record, he was known. He might have been tight-lipped about his operation, but somewhere somebody was going to know something.

One thing. That's all we needed. You could start with dead men, all right, but it won't do you any good if they only lead to other dead men. Mr. Dickerson had played some smart cards. He had picked his people well. The ones here were clean. The ones who weren't were dead. The hoods in town could be taken in and questioned, but if they knew nothing because the orders hadn't been issued yet, they couldn't say anything. It was still a free country and you couldn't make them leave the state as long as they stayed clean. The men behind them were power who could still turn on the heat through odd but important channels so you couldn't roust them too far.

I told Pat I'd see him sometime after lunch, walked him downstairs, left a key with the super, and gave him a fin for his trouble. Pat went on downtown and I hopped a cab across town to Annette Lee's place, got the landlady to let me in, and stepped into her living room.

The old gal was still in her rocker, still going through that same perpetual rhythm, stopping only when her chair had inched against another piece of furniture. Her curtains were drawn back, letting in the early light, and she smiled a big hello when she saw me.

"How nice of you to come back, young man," she said. She held out her hand without getting up and I took it. "Sit down, please."

I tossed my hat on a table and pulled up another straight-back chair and perched on the end of it.

"Your young lady was here yesterday. We had a lovely visit. It isn't often I get company, you know."

I said, "She mentioned you wanted to see me."

"Yes." Annette Lee nodded, then leaned her head back against the chair with her eyes half shut. "We were talking. I . . ." She waved her hand vaguely in front of her face. "Sometimes I forget things. I'm going on ninety now. I think I've lived too long already."

"You never live too long."

"Perhaps so. I can still enjoy things. I can dream. Do you dream, Mr. . . . ?"

"Hammer."

"Mr. Hammer. Do you dream?"

"Sometimes."

"You're not old enough to dream back like I do. It's something like being reborn. I like to dream. They were good days then. I dream about them because they're all I have to dream about. Yes, they were fine days."

"What was it you wanted to tell me, Miss Lee?" I asked her gently.

"Oh?" She thought a moment, then: "There was something. Your young lady and I talked about Sally and Sue. Yes, that was it. Dear Sally, she was so lovely. It was a pity she died."

"Miss Lee . . ."

"Yes?"

"The night she died . . . do you remember it well?"

"Oh yes. Oh yes indeed." Her rocking slowed momentarily so she could shift positions, then started again.

"Was she drunk, really drunk?"

"Dear me, yes. Sally drank all the time. From very early in the morning. There was nothing I could do so I tried to keep her company and talk to her. She didn't want to talk too much, you know. When she did it was drunk talk I couldn't always understand. Do you know what I mean?"

"I've heard it."

"There was that thing with the snakes you mentioned. It was rather an obsession with her."

"She was frightened of the snake?"

Annette Lee lifted her head and peered at me. "No, that was the strange thing. She wasn't afraid. It was . . . well, she hated it."

"Was the snake a person?"

"Excuse me?"

"Could she have been referring to a person as The Snake? Not snakes or a snake. *The Snake.*"

The rocking stopped completely. She looked at me curiously in the semi-darkened room, her fingertip touching her lips. "So that was what she meant."

"Go on."

"No wonder I didn't understand. My goodness, I never understood in all this time. Yes, she said *the* snake. It was always *the* snake. She hated *the* snake, that was why she wanted to live so far away from the city. She never wanted to go back."

"Annette . . . who was Sue's father?"

The old girl made a face at me and raised the thin line of her eyebrows. "Does it matter?"

"It might."

"But I'm afraid I couldn't tell you."

"Why not?"

"Simply because I don't know. Sue has Sally's maiden name, you know. She never got her father's name because she doesn't know who he is. I'm afraid Sally was . . . a bit promiscuous. She had many men and among them would be Sue's father. I doubt if Sally ever really knew either. A pity. Sue was such a lovely baby."

"Could it have been Blackie Conley?"

For the first time Annette Lee giggled. "Dear no. Not him. Never Blackie."

"Why?"

"Simply because he wasn't capable. I think that was one of the reasons Blackie was so . . . so frustrated. He *did* like the ladies, you know. He slept with one after the other. He even married two of them but it never worked out. He always wanted an heir but he wasn't capable. Why . . . the boys used to kid him about it."

Her feet pushed harder until she had to edge the chair away from the wall so that she faced me more directly. "Do you ever remember Bud Packer?"

"Just the name."

"Bud was . . . joshing him one day about his . . . impotence and Blackie shot him. You know where. I think Blackie did time for that but I don't rightly remember. No, Blackie was not Sue's father by any means. Besides, you're forgetting one big thing."

I let her say it.

"Blackie's been gone . . . for years. Long before Sue was born. Blackie is dead somewhere."

She put her head back and closed her eyes. I said, "Tired?"

110

"No, just thinking. Daydreaming."

"How about this angle . . . could Sim Torrence have been the father?"

Her giggle broke into a soft cackle only the old can make. "Sim Torrence? I'm afraid not. Sue was born before they were married."

"He could still be the father."

"You don't understand, Mr. . . ."

"Hammer."

"Mr. Hammer. You see, I was with Sally always before. I knew the many faces she was with. I know who she slept with and none of them were Sim Torrence. It wasn't until after the baby was born that they were married when he took her in and provided for them." The flat laugh came out again. "Those two could never have a baby of their own though."

"Why not?"

"Because she and Sim never slept together. After the baby was born Sally never let a man near her. She underwent a change. All she thought of was the baby, making plans for her, hoping for her to grow up and be somebody. You know, I hate to give away women-secrets, but Sally deliberately cultivated Sim Torrence. They knew each other for some time earlier. Some court case. She managed to meet him somehow and I remember them going out for a couple of weeks before she brought him to our apartment and told me they were going to get married."

"Did Torrence take it well?"

"How does any man take it who is going to lose his bachelorhood?" She smiled knowingly. "He was rather shaken. Almost embarrassed. But he did provide well for Sally and Sue. They had a simple ceremony and moved into his town house."

"Were you with them?"

"Oh yes. Sally wouldn't leave me. Why, I was the only one who could take care of her and the baby. She wasn't very domestic, you know. She wasn't supposed to be. Yes, those were different women then. Showgirls. They had to be pampered."

"Why wouldn't she let Torrence near her in bed?"

"Does it sound strange that a woman who was a . . . a

111

whore would be afraid of sex?"

I shook my head. "Most of them are frigid anyway," I said bluntly.

"So true, so true. Well, that was Sally. Frigid. Having the baby scared her. Even having a man scared her."

"Was she scared of Torrence?"

"Of every man, Mr. . . . ," and this time she remembered my name and smiled, ". . . Hammer. Yes, Sim Torrence scared her but I think he understood. He let her stay at that place in the country. He came up on occasions and it was very strained but he was very understanding about it too. Of course, like all men, he could bury himself in his work. That was his real wife, his work."

"Miss Lee . . . the last time I was here we talked about Blackie Conley, remember?"

"I remember."

"You said you knew about the plans he made for that robbery he and Sonny Motley were involved in. What were they?"

She stopped rocking, her face curious again. "Are you looking for the money?"

"I'm a cop, Miss Lee. I'm looking for a killer, for the money . . . for anything that will help keep trouble from Sue."

"Sue? But that was before she was born."

"It can come back to hurt her. Now what did you hear?"

She nodded, pressing her lips together, her hands grasping the arms of the rockers. "Do you really think . . . ?"

"It might help."

"I see." She paused, thought a moment, then said, "You know that Sonny really didn't plan the robbery. It was his gang, but he didn't plan it. They were . . . acting for someone."

"I know about that."

"Blackie had instructions to find a place where they were going to hide out. He was told where to go and how to do it. I remember because I listened to the call." She chuckled at the thought. "I never did like Blackie. He was at Sally's place when he took the call. In fact, that was where they did all their planning, at Sally's apartment. Sonny was going with her then when she wasn't sneaking off with Blackie."

"I see."

"Really," she told me, "I wasn't supposed to know about these things. I was always in the other room out of sight, but I was worried about Sally and tried to find out what was going on. I listened in and they didn't know it."

"None of this came out at the trial," I reminded her.

"Nor was it about to, young man. I didn't want to involve Sally any more than she was. She *did* appear in court, you know."

"Briefly. She wasn't implicated. She was treated as an innocent victim."

Those watery old eyes found mine and laughed in their depths. "No, Sally wasn't so innocent. She knew everything that went on. Sally's pose was very deliberate. Very deliberate. She was a better actress than anyone imagined."

Annette Lee leaned forward like some old conspirator. "Now that it can't hurt her, let me tell you something. It was through dear Sally that this robbery came about. All arrangements, all contacts were made through her. Sonny was quite a man in those days and ran a sizable operation. But it was through Sally Devon that another party interested Sonny in that robbery. No, Sally was hardly the innocent victim."

I didn't let her see me take it in. I passed it off quickly to get her back on the track again, but now the angles were starting to show. I said, "When Blackie Conley got this call . . . what happened?"

Jerked suddenly from one train of thought, she sat back frowning. "Oh . . . Blackie . . . well, I heard this voice . . ."

"A man?"

"Yes. He told Blackie to see a man in a certain real estate agency, one that could be trusted. He gave him the phone number."

I added, "And Blackie arranged to rent a house in the Catskills?"

"That's right. He made the call right then and said he'd be in the next day." She opened her eyes again, now her fingers tapping a silent tune on the chair. "But then he made another call to Howie Green."

"Who?"

"Howie Green. He was a bootlegger, dearie, but he owned properties here in the city. He invested his money wisely, Howie did, and always had something to show for it. Howie was as crooked as they come, but smarter than most of them. One of Howie's enterprises was a real estate agency that used to be someplace on Broadway. Oh yes, Howie was a big man, but he owed Blackie Conley a favor. Blackie killed a man for Howie and held it over his head. He told Howie he wanted a place to hole up in somewhere away from the city and to pick it out."

"Where was it, Annette?"

"I don't know, young man. Howie merely said he'd do it for him. That was all. I suppose Blackie took care of it later. However, it's all over now. Howie Green's dead too. He died in an accident not long afterward."

"Before the robbery?"

"I really don't remember that."

I reached for my hat and stood up. "You've been a great help, Annette."

"Have I really?"

I nodded.

"Will Sue be . . . all right?"

"I'm sure she will."

"Someday," she asked me, "will you bring her to me? I would like to see her again."

"We'll make a point of it."

"Good-by then. It was nice of you to come over."

"My pleasure, Miss Lee."

At two o'clock I contacted Pat and made a date to meet him at his office. He didn't like the idea because he knew Grebb would want to sit in on the conversation but thought he could arrange it so we could be alone.

I took a cab downtown, found Pat alone at his desk buried in the usual paperwork, waited for him to finish, then said, "What officers were in on the Motley holdup? Any still around?"

"This your day for surprises?"

"Hit me."

114

"Inspector Grebb was one. He was a beat cop who was alerted for the action."

"Oh hell."

"Why?"

"Think he'd remember the details?"

"I don't remember Grebb ever forgetting anything."

"Then let's call him in."

"You sure about this?" Pat asked me.

"It's the easy way. So we give him a bite after all."

Pat nodded, lifted the phone, and made a call. When he hung up he said, "The Inspector will be happy to see you."

"I bet."

It didn't take him long to get up there. He didn't have Charlie Force with him either. He came in with the patient attitude of the professional cop, always ready to wait, always ready to act when the time came. He might have been a tough, sour old apple, but he made it the hard way and you couldn't take it away from him.

Inwardly I laughed at myself because if I wasn't careful I could almost like him.

"Whose party is it this time?" he asked.

Pat said, "He's throwing it."

"I never thought you'd ask, Hammer." He dragged a chair out with his foot, sat in it heavily and sighed, but it was all an act. He was no more tired or bored than I was. "Shoot," he said.

"Pat tells me you were in on the Motley thing thirty years ago."

"My second day on the beat, Hammer. That shows you how close to retirement I am. My present job is a gratuity. One last fling for the old dog in a department he always wanted to run."

"Better luck in your next one."

"We aren't talking about that. What's with the Motley job?"

"How did the cops get wise?"

"Why don't you read the transcript of the trial? It was mentioned."

"This is easier. Besides, I wanted to be sure."

Grebb pulled a cigar from his pocket, snapped off the end, and fired it up. "Like a lot of big ones that went bust," he said, "somebody pulled the cork. The

115

department got a call. It went through the D.A.'s office."

"Torrence?"

"No, one of the others got it and passed it to him. Torrence handled it personally though."

"Where were you?"

"Staked out where the truck was hidden in case they got through somehow. They never made it. We got the truck and the driver. Second day on the beat too, I'll never forget it. Fresh out of school, still hardly shaving, and I get a hot one right off. Made me decide to stay in the department."

"How long did you have to get ready?"

"About an hour, if I remember right. It was plenty of time. We could have done it in fifteen minutes."

"They ever find out who made the call?"

"Nope."

"They look very hard?"

Grebb just shrugged noncommittally. Then he said, "Let's face it, we'd sooner have stoolies on the outside where they can call these things in than a live guy testifying in court who winds up a dead squealer a day later. We didn't break our backs running down anybody. Whoever it was played it the way we liked it. The job was a bust and we nailed the crew."

"It wasn't a bust, Inspector."

He stared at me until his face hurt.

"Nobody ever located the money."

"That's happened before. One of those things."

"Blackie Conley simply disappeared."

The cigar bobbed in his mouth. "And if he lived very long afterward he's a better man than I am. By now he'd be dead anyway." He took the cigar away from his mouth and flipped the ash off with his pinky. "But let's get back to the money . . . that's the interesting part."

"I have an idea it might show up."

"Maybe we better listen to your idea."

"Uh-uh. Facts I'll give you, ideas stay in my pocket until I can prove them out."

"Facts then."

"None you don't already have if you want to check the transcript like you suggested. I just make something different out of them, that's all."

Grebb put the cigar back between his teeth and pushed

himself out of his chair. When he was on his feet he glanced at Pat meaningfully, said, "Don't let me wait too long, Captain," then went out.

"I wish you'd quit pushing him," Pat told me. "Now what's with this bit?"

I sat in the chair Grebb had vacated and propped my feet on Pat's desk. "I think Blackie Conley's alive."

"How'd he do it?"

"He was the planner behind the operation. He set it up, then phoned in a double-cross. Trouble was, he should have cut it shorter. He almost lost it himself. He laid out one escape plan, but took an alternate. He got away in that cab with the three million bucks and sat on it someplace."

Pat tapped a pencil on the desk as I gave him the information Annette Lee gave me. Every once in a while he'd make a note on a pad, study it, then make another.

"We'll have to locate whatever records are left of Howie Green's business. If he was dealing in real estate it will be a matter of public record."

"You don't think Blackie would use his own name, do you?"

"We can narrow it down. Look, check your file on Green."

Pat put in another call and for the twenty minutes it took to get the papers up we went over the angles of the case. I still wouldn't lay it out the way I saw it, but he had enough to reach the same conclusion if he thought the same way.

The uniformed officer handed Pat a yellowed folder and Pat opened it on his desk. Howie Green, deceased. Known bootlegger, six arrests, two minor convictions. Suspected of duplicity in a murder of one Francis Gorman, another bootlegger who moved into his territory. Charge dropped. Known to have large holdings that were legally acquired as far as the law could prove. His annual income made him a rich man for the times. He was killed by a hit-and-run driver not far from his own house and the date given was three days before the robbery of the three million bucks.

"Pretty angle, Pat."

"Spell it out."

"If Conley did get hideout property from Green, paid for it, made the transaction, and accepted the papers in a phony name and took possession, then killed him before Green knew what he wanted it for, who could say where he was? Chances were that nobody but Conley and Green ever saw each other and Green wasn't around to talk any more."

Pat closed the folder and shoved it in his desk. "We could check all the transactions Green made in the few weeks prior to his death."

"Time, buddy. We haven't got the time."

"But I have one thing you don't have."

I knew what he was going to say.

"Men. We can put enough troops on it to shorten the time."

"It'll still be a long job."

"You know a better way?"

The phone rang before I could answer and although I could hear the hurried chatter at the other end I couldn't make it out. When he cradled the phone Pat said, "One of my squad in Brooklyn on that Levitt run-down."

"Oh?"

"He was eating with one of the men from the precinct over there when a call came in about a body. He went along with his friend and apparently the dead guy is one of the ones he showed Basil Levitt's picture to."

"A starter," I said.

"Could be. Want to take a run over?"

"Why not?"

Pat got his car from the lot and we hopped in, cutting over the bridge into the Brooklyn section. The address was in the heart of Flatbush, one block off the Avenue, a neighborhood bar and grill that was squeezed in between a grocery and a dry-cleaning place.

A squad car was at the curb and a uniformed patrolman stood by the door. Two more, obviously detectives from the local precinct, were in the doorway talking. Pat knew the Lieutenant in charge, shook hands with him, introduced him to me as Joe Cavello, then went inside.

Squatting nervously on a stool, the bartender watched us, trying to be casual about the whole thing. Lieutenant

118

Cavello nodded toward him and said, "He found the body."

"When?"

"About an hour ago. He had to go down to hook into some fresh beer kegs and found the guy on the floor. He'd been shot once in the head with a small-caliber gun . . . I'd say about a .32."

"The M.E. set the time of death?" I asked him.

"About twelve to fifteen hours. He'll be more specific after an autopsy."

"Who was he?" Pat said.

"The owner of the place."

"You know him?"

"Somewhat," Cavello said. "We've had him down to the precinct a few times. Twice on wife beating and another when he was picked up in a raid on a card game. This is kind of a chintzy joint. Local bums hang out here because the drinks are cheap. But that's all they sell anyway, cheap booze. We've had a few complaints about some fights in here but nothing ever happened. You know, the usual garbage that goes with these slop chutes."

Pat said, "I had Nelson and Kiley over here doing a rundown on Basil Levitt. You hear about it?"

"Yeah, Lew Nelson checked in with me right after it happened. He saw the body. It was the guy he spoke to all right. I asked around but nobody here seemed to know Levitt."

"How about the bartender?" I said.

Cavello shook his head. "Nothing there. He does the day work and nothing more. When the boss came on, he went off. He doesn't know the night crowd at all."

"He live around here?"

"Red Hook. Not his neighborhood here and he couldn't care less."

While Pat went over the details of what the police picked up I wandered back to the end of the bar. There was a back room used as a storeroom and a place for the food locker with a doorway to one side that opened into the cellar. The lights were on downstairs and I went down to the spot behind the stairs where the chalk

119

marks outlined the position of the body. They were half on the floor and half on the wall, so the guy was found in a sitting position.

Back upstairs Cavello had taken Pat to the end of the bar and I got back in on the conversation. Cavello said, "Near as we could figure it out, this guy Thomas Kline closed the bar earlier than usual, making the few customers he had leave. It was something he had never done before apparently. He'd stick it out if there was a dime in the joint left to be spent. This time he bitched about a headache, closed up, and shut off the lights. That was it. We spoke to the ones who were here then, but they all went off to another place and closed it down much later, then went home. Clean alibis. All working men for a change. No records.

"We think he met somebody here for some purpose. Come here." He led the way to a table in one corner and pointed to the floor. A small stain showed against the oiled wood. "Blood. It matched the victim's. Here's where he was shot. The killer took the body downstairs, dumped it behind the staircase where it couldn't be seen very easily, then left. The door locks by simply closing it so it was simple enough to do. One block down he's in traffic, and anyplace along the Avenue he could have picked up a cab if he didn't have his own car. We're checking all the cabbies' sheets now."

But I had stopped listening to him about then. I was looking at the back corner of the wall. I tapped Pat on the arm and pointed. "You remember the call you got from someone inquiring about Levitt?"

"Yeah," he said.

There was an open pay phone on the wall about four feet away from a jukebox.

Pat walked over to it, looked at the records on the juke, but who could tell rock-and-roll from the titles? He said to Cavello, "Many places got these open phones?"

"Sure," Cavello told him, "most of the spots that haven't got room for a booth. Mean anything?"

"I don't know. It could."

"Anything I could help with?"

Pat explained the situation and Cavello said he'd try to find anyone who saw Kline making a phone call about that time. He didn't expect much luck though.

120

People in that neighborhood didn't talk too freely to the police. It was more likely that they wouldn't remember anything rather than get themselves involved.

Another plainclothes officer came in then, said hello to Pat, and he introduced me to Lew Nelson. He didn't have anything to add to the story and so far that day hadn't found anybody who knew much about Levitt at all.

I tapped his shoulder and said, "How did Kline react when you showed him Levitt's photo?"

"Well, he jumped a little. He said he couldn't be sure and I figured he was lying. I got the same reaction from others beside him. That Levitt was a mean son and I don't think anybody wanted to mess around with him. He wanted to know what he was wanted for and I wouldn't say anything except that he was dead and he seemed pretty satisfied at that.

"Tell you one thing. That guy was thinking of something. He studied that photo until he was sure he knew him and then told me he never saw him before. Maybe he thought he had an angle somewhere."

There wasn't much left there for us. Pat left a few instructions, sent Nelson back on the streets again, and started outside. He stopped for a final word to Cavello so I went on alone and stood on the sidewalk beside the cop on guard there. It wasn't until he went to answer the radio in the squad car that I saw the thing his position had obscured.

In the window of the bar was a campaign poster and on it a full-face picture of a smiling Torrence who was running in the primaries for governor and under it was the slogan, *WIN WITH SIM*.

CHAPTER NINE

I made the call from the drugstore on the corner. I dialed the Torrence estate and waited while the phone rang a half-dozen times, each time feeling the cold go through me deeper and deeper.

Damn, it couldn't be too late!

Then a sleepy voice said, "Yes?" and there was no worry in it at all.

"Geraldine?"

"Mike, you thing you."

"Look . . ."

"Why did you leave me? How could you leave me?"

"I'll tell you later. Has Torrence come home yet?"

My voice startled her into wakefulness. "But . . . no, he's due here in an hour though. He called this morning from Albany to tell me when he'd be home."

"Good, no listen. Is Sue all right?"

"Yes . . . she's still in bed. I gave her another seda-tive."

"Well, get her out of it. Both of you hop in a car and get out of there. Now . . . not later, now."

"But, Mike . . ."

"Damn it, shut up and do what I say. There's going to be trouble I can't explain."

"Where can we go? Mike, I don't . . ."

I gave her my new address and added, "Go right there and stay there. The super has the key and will let you in. Don't open that door for anybody until you're sure it's me, understand? I can't tell you any more except that your neck and Sue's neck are out a mile. We have another dead man on our hands and we don't need any more. You got that?"

She knew I wasn't kidding. There was too much stark urgency in my voice. She said she'd leave in a few minutes and when she did I could sense the fear that touched her.

I tapped the receiver cradle down, broke the connection, dropped in a dime, and dialed my own number. Velda came on after the first ring with a guarded hello.

I said, "It's breaking, baby. How do you feel?"

122

"Not too bad. I can get around."

"Swell. You go downstairs and tell the super that a Geraldine King and Sue Devon are to be admitted to my apartment. Nobody else. Let him keep the key. Then you get down to Sim Torrence's headquarters and check up on his movements all day yesterday. I want every minute of the day spelled out and make it as specific as you can. He got a phone call yesterday. See if it originated from there. I don't care if he took ten minutes out to go to the can . . . you find out about it. I'm chiefly interested in any time he took off last night."

"Got it, Mike. Where can I reach you?"

"At the apartment. When I get through I'll go right there. Shake it up."

"Chop chop. Love me?"

"What a time to ask."

"Well?"

"Certainly, you nut."

She laughed that deep, throaty laugh and hung up on me and I had a quick picture of her sliding out of bed, those beautiful long legs rippling into a body . . . oh hell.

I put the phone back and went back to Pat.

"Where'd you go?" he said.

"We got a killer, buddy."

He froze for a second. "You didn't find anything?"

"No? Then make sense out of this." I pointed to the picture of Sim Torrence in the window.

"Go ahead."

"Sim's on the way up. He's getting where he always wanted to be. He's got just one bug in his life and that's the kid, Sue Devon. All her life she's been on his back about something in their past and there was always that chance she might find it.

"One time he defended a hard case and when he needed one he called on the guy. Basil Levitt. He wanted Sue knocked off. Some instinct told Sue what he intended to do and she ran for it and wound up at Velda's. She didn't know it, but it was already too late. Levitt was on her tail all the while, followed her, set up in a place opposite the house, and waited for her to show.

"The trouble was, Velda was in hiding too. She
123

respected the kid's fears and kept her under cover until she was out of trouble herself, then she would have left the place with her. Hell, Pat, Levitt didn't come in there for Velda . . . he was after the kid. When he saw me he must have figured Torrence sent somebody else because he was taking too long and he wasn't about to lose his contract money. That's why Levitt bust in like that.

"Anyway, when Torrence made the deal he must have met Levitt in this joint here thinking he'd never be recognized. But he forgot that his picture is plastered all over on posters throughout the city. Maybe Kline never gave it a thought if he recognized him then. Maybe Kline only got the full picture when he saw Levitt's photo. But he put the thing together. First he called your department for information and grew suspicious when nobody gave him anything concrete.

"Right here he saw Torrence over a barrel so yesterday he called him and told him to meet him. Sim must have jumped out of his skin. He dummied an excuse and probably even led into a trip to Albany for further cover . . . this we'll know about when I see Velda. But he got here all right. He saw Kline and that was the last Kline saw of anything."

"You think too much, Mike."

"The last guy that said that is dead." I grinned.

"We'd better get up there then."

New York, when the traffic is thick, is a maddening place. From high above the streets the cars look like a winding line of ants, but when you are in the convoy it becomes a raucous noise, a composite of horns and engines and voices cursing at other voices. It's a heavy smell of exhaust fumes and unburned hydrocarbons and in the desire to compress time and space the distance between cars is infinitesimal.

The running lights designed to keep traffic moving at a steady pace seem to break down then. They all become red. Always, there is a bus or truck ahead, or an out-of-town driver searching for street signs. There are pedestrians who take their time, sometimes deliberately blocking the lights in the never-ceasing battle against the enemy, those who are mounted.

In the city the average speed of a fire truck breaks down to eighteen miles an hour with all its warning devices going, so imagine what happens to time and distance when the end-of-day rush is on. Add to that the rain that fogged the windshields and made every sudden stop hazardous.

Ordinarily from Brooklyn the Torrence place would have been an hour away. But not this night. No, this was a special night of delay and frustration, and if Pat hadn't been able to swing around two barriers with his badge held out the window it would have been an hour longer still.

It was a quarter to eight when we turned in the street Sim Torrence lived on. Behind the wall and the shrubbery I could see lights on in the house and outside that there was no activity at all. From the end of the street, walking toward us, was the patrolman assigned to the beat on special duty, and when we stopped his pace quickened so that he was there when we got out.

Pat held his badge out again, but the cop recognized me. Pat said, "Everything all right here?"

"Yes, sir. Miss King and the girl left some time ago and Torrence arrived, but there has been no trouble. Anything I can help with?"

"No, just routine. We have to see Torrence."

"Sure. He left the gate open."

We left the car on the street and walked in, staying on the grass. I had the .45 in my hand and Pat had his Police Positive out and ready. Sim Torrence's Cadillac was parked in front of the door and when I felt it the hood was still warm.

Both of us knew what to do. We checked the windows and the back, met again around the front, then I went up to the door while Pat stood by in the shadows.

I touched the buzzer and heard the chime from inside.

Nobody answered so I did it again.

I didn't bother for a third try. I reached out, leaned against the door latch, and it swung in quietly. I went in first, Pat right behind me covering the blind spots. First I motioned him to be quiet, then to follow me since I knew the layout.

There was a deathly stillness about the house that
125

didn't belong there. With all the lights that were going there should have been some sort of sound. But there was nothing.

We checked through the downstairs room, opening closets and probing behind the furniture. Pat looked across the room at me, shook his head, and I pointed toward the stairs.

The master bedroom was the first door on the right. The door was partly open and there was a light on there too. We took that one first.

And that was where we found Sim Torrence. He wasn't winning any more.

He lay face down on the floor with a bullet through his head and a puddle of blood running away from him like juice from a stepped-on tomato. We didn't stop there. We went into every room in the house looking for a killer before we finally came back to Sim.

Pat wrapped the phone in a handkerchief, called the local department, and reported in. When he hung up he said, "You know we're in a sling, don't you?"

"Why?"

"We should have called in from Brooklyn and let them cover it from this end."

"My foot, buddy. Getting in a jam won't help anything. As far as anyone is concerned we came up here on a social call. I was here last night helping out during an emergency and I came back to check, that's all."

"And what about the women?"

"We'll get to them before anybody else will."

"You'd better be right."

"Quit worrying."

While we waited we checked the area around the body for anything that might tie in with the murder. There were no spent cartridges so we both assumed the killer used a revolver. I prowled around the house looking for a sign of entry, since Geraldine would have locked the door going out and Sim behind him, coming in. The killer must have already been here and made his own entry the easy way through the front door.

The sirens were screaming up the street outside when I found out where he got in. The window in Sue's room had been neatly jimmied from the trellis outside and

126

was a perfect, quiet entry into the house. Anybody could have come over the walls without being seen by the lone cop on the beat. From there up that solid trellis was as easy as taking the steps.

Sue's bed was still rumpled. Geraldine must have literally dragged her out of it because the burned stuffed toy was still there crammed under the covers, almost like a body itself.

Then I could see that something new had been added. There was a bullet hole and powder burns on the sheet and when I flipped it back I saw the hole drilled into the huge toy.

Somebody had mistaken that charred ruin for Sue under the covers and tried to put a bullet through her!

Back to Lolita again. Damn, where would it end?

What kind of a person were we dealing with?

I went to put the covers back in their original position before calling Pat in when I saw the stuffed bear up close for the first time. It had been her mother's and the fire had burned it stiff. The straw sticking out was hard and crisp with age, the ends black from the heat. During the night Sue must have lain on it and her weight split open a seam.

An edge of a letter stuck out of it.

I tugged it loose, didn't bother to look at it then because they were coming in downstairs now, racing up the stairs. I stuck the letter in my pocket and called for Pat.

He got the import of it right away but didn't say anything. From all appearances this was a break-in and anybody could have done it. The implications were too big to let the thing out now and he wasn't going to do much explaining until we had time to go over it.

The reporters had already gathered and were yelling for admittance. Tomorrow this kill would make every headline in the country and the one in Brooklyn would be lucky if it got a squib in any sheet at all. There was going to be some high-level talk before this one broke straight and Pat knew it too.

It was an hour before we got out of there and back in the car. Some of the bigwigs of the political party had arrived and were being pressed by the reporters, but they had nothing to say. They got in on VIP status and were immediately sent into the den to be quizzed by the officers in charge and as long as there was plenty to do we could ride for a while.

Pat didn't speak until we were halfway back to the city, then all he said was, "One of your theories went out the window today."

"Which one?"

"If Sim planned to kill Sue, how would he excuse it?"

"I fell into that one with no trouble, Pat," I said. "You know how many times he has been threatened?"

"I know."

"So somebody was trying to get even. Revenge motive. They hit the kid."

"But Sue is still alive."

"Somebody thought he got her tonight. I'll tell you this . . . I bet the first shot fired was into that bed. The killer turned on the light to make sure and saw what happened. He didn't dare let it stand like that so he waited around. Then in came Sim. Now it could be passed off as a burglary attempt while the real motive gets lost in the rush."

I tapped his arm. "There's one other thing too. The night of the first try there were two groups. Levitt and Kid Hand. They weren't working together and they were both after the same thing . . . the kid."

"All right, sharpie, what's the answer?"

"I think it's going to be three million bucks," I said.

"You have more than that to sell."

"There's Blackie Conley."

"And you think he's got the money?"

"Want to bet?"

"Name it."

"A night on the town. A foursome. We'll find you a broad. Loser picks up all the tabs."

Pat nodded. "You got it, but forget finding me a broad. I'll get my own."

"You'll probably bring a policewoman."

"With you around it wouldn't be a bad idea," he said.

He let me out in front of my apartment and I promised to call him as soon as I heard from Velda. He was going to run the Torrence thing through higher channels and let them handle this hotcake.

I went upstairs, called through the door, and let Geraldine open it. Velda still hadn't gotten back. Sue was inside on the couch, awake, but still drowsy from the sedatives she had taken. I made Geraldine sit down next to her, then broke the news.

At first Sue didn't react. Finally she said, "He's really dead?"

"Really, sugar."

Somehow a few years seemed to drape themselves around her. She looked at the floor, made a wry face, and shrugged. "I'm sorry, Mike. I don't feel anything. Just free. I feel free."

Geraldine looked like she was about to break, but she came through it. There was a stricken expression in her eyes and her mouth hung slackly. She kept repeating, "Oh, no!" over and over again and that was all. When she finally accepted it she asked, "Who, Mike, who did it?"

"We don't know."

"This is terrible. The whole political . . ."

"It's more terrible than that, kid. Politicians can always be replaced. I suggest you contact your office when you feel up to it. There's going to be hell to pay and if your outfit gets into power this time it'll be by a miracle . . . and those days, believe me, are over."

She started asking me something else, but the phone rang and I jumped to answer it. Velda said, "Mike . . . I just heard. Is it true?"

"He's had it. What did you come up with?"

"About the time you mentioned . . . nobody could account for Torrence's whereabouts for almost two hours. Nobody really looked for him and they all supposed he was with somebody else, but nobody could clear him for that time."

"That does it then. Come on back."

"Twenty minutes."

"Shake it."

In a little while I was going to be tied in with this mess and would be getting plenty of visitors and I didn't want either Geraldine or Sue around. Their time would come, but not right now. I called a hotel, made reservations for them both, dialed for a cab, and told them to get ready. Neither wanted to leave until I told them there was no choice. I wanted them completely out of sight and told Geraldine to stay put again, having her meals sent up until I called for her.

Events had moved too quickly and she couldn't think for herself any longer. She agreed dumbly, the girls got into their coats, and I walked them out to the cab.

Upstairs I sat at the desk and took the letter out of my pocket. Like the straw, it was crisp with age, but still sealed, and after all these years smelled faintly of some feminine perfume. I slid my finger under the flap and opened it.

The handwriting was the scrawl of a drunk trying hard for sobriety. The lines were uneven and ran to the edge of the page, but it was legible enough.

It read:

Darling Sue:

My husband Sim is the one we called The Snake. Hate him, darling, because he wants us dead. Be careful of him. Someday he will try to kill us both. Sim Torrence could prove I helped deliver narcotics at one time. He could have sent me to prison. We made a deal that I was to be the go-between for him and Sonny Motley and he was going to arrange the robbery. He could do it because he knew every detail of the money exchange. What he really wanted was for Sonny and the rest to be caught so he could boost his career. That happened, didn't it, darling? He never should have left me out in the cold. After I had you I wanted security for you and knew how to get it. I didn't love Sim Torrence. He hated me like he hates anybody in his way. I made him do it for you, dearest. I will hide this letter where he won't find it but you will someday. He searches everything I have to be sure this can't happen. Be careful my darling. He is The Snake and he will try to kill you if he can. Be careful of accidents. He will have to make it look like one.

All My Love,
Mother

The Snake . . . the one thing they all feared . . . and now he was dead. Dedicated old Win with Sim, an en-

130

gineer of robberies, hirer of murderers, a killer himself
. . . what a candidate for governor. The people would
never know how lucky they were.

The Snake. A good name for him. I was right . . . it
worked the way I figured it. The votes weren't all
counted yet, but the deck was stacked against Sim Torrence. In death he was going to take a fall bigger than
the one he would have taken in life.

Torrence never got the three million. He never gave
a damn about it in the first place. All breaking up that
robbery did was earn him prestige and some political
titles. It was his first step into the big-time and he made
it himself. He put everybody's life on the block including
his own and swung it. I wondered what plans he had
made for Sally if she hadn't nipped into him first. In
fact, marrying her was even a good deal for him. It
gave him a chance to keep her under wraps and lay
the groundwork for a murder.

Hell, if I could check back that far with accuracy I
knew what I would find. Sim paid the house upstate a
visit, found Annette Lee asleep and Sally in a dead drunk.
He simply dragged her out into the winter night and the
weather did the rest. He couldn't have done anything
with the kid right then without starting an investigation.
Sally would have been a tragic accident; the kid too
meant trouble.

So he waited. Like a good father, which added to his
political image, he adopted her into his house. When
it was not expedient for him to have her around any
longer he arranged for her execution through Levitt.
He sure was a lousy planner there. Levitt talked too
much. Enough to die before he could do the job.

In one way Sue forced her own near-death with her
crazy behavior. Whatever she couldn't get out of her
mind were the things her mother told her repeatedly in
her drunken moods. It had an effect all right. She made
it clear to Sim that he was going to have to kill her if
he didn't want her shooting her mouth off.

Sim would have known who The Snake was. Sally
had referred to him by that often enough. No wonder
he ducked it at the trial. No wonder it seared him silly
when Sue kept insisting her mother left something for
her to read. No wonder he searched her things. That

131

last time in Sue's little house was one of desperation. He knew that sooner or later something would come to light and if it happened he was politically dead, which to him was death *in toto*.

But somebody made a mistake. There was a bigger snake loose than Torrence ever was. There was a snake with three million bucks buried in its hole and that could be the worst kind of snake of all. Hell, Sim wasn't a snake at all. He was a goddamn worm.

I folded the letter and put it back in my pocket when the bell rang. When I opened the door Velda folded into my arms like a big cat, kicked it shut with her heel, and buried her face against my neck.

"You big slob," she said.

While she made coffee I told her about it, taking her right through from the beginning. She read the letter twice, getting the full implication of it all.

"Does Pat know all this?"

"Not yet. He'd better take first things first."

"What are you going to do?"

"Call Art Rickerby."

I picked the unlisted number out of memory and got Art on the phone. It took a full thirty minutes to rehash the entire situation, but he listened patiently, letting me get it across. It was the political side of it he was more concerned with at the moment, realizing what propaganda ammunition the other side could use against us.

One thing about truth . . . let it shine and you were all right. It was the lies that could hurt you. But there were ways of letting the truth come out so as to nullify the awkward side of it and this was what the striped-pants boys were for.

Art said he'd get into it right away, but only because of my standing as a representative of the agency he was part of.

I said, "Where do I go from here, Art?"

"Now who's going to tell you, big man?"

"It isn't over yet."

"It's never over, Mike. When this is over there will be something else."

"There will be some big heat coming my way. I'd hate to lose my pretty little ticket. It's all I have."

He was silent for a moment, then he said, "I'll let

you in on a confidence. There are people here who like you. We can't all operate the same way. Put a football player on the diamond and he'd never get around the bases. A baseball player in the middle of a pileup would never get up. You've never been a total unknown and now that you're back, stay back. When we need you, we'll yell. Meanwhile nobody's going to pick up your ticket as long as you stay clean enough. I didn't say legal . . . I said clean. One day we'll talk some more about this, but not now. You do what you have to do. Just remember that everybody's watching so make it good."

"Great, all I have to do is stay alive."

"Well, if you do get knocked off, let me repeat a favorite old saying of yours, '*Kismet, buddy.*' "

He hung up and left me staring at the phone. I grinned, then put it down and started to laugh. Velda said, "What's so funny?"

"I don't know," I told her. "It's just funny. Grebb and Charlie Force are going to come at me like tigers when this is over to get my official status changed and if I can make it work they don't have a chance."

That big, beautiful thing walked over next to me and slid her arms around my waist and said, "They never did have a chance. You're the tiger, man."

I turned around slowly and ran my hands under her sweater, up the warm flesh of her back. She pulled herself closer to me so that every curve of hers matched my own and her breasts became rigid against my chest.

There was a tenderness to her mouth that was only at the beginning, then her lips parted with a gentle searching motion and her tongue flicked at mine with the wordless gestures of love. Somehow the couch was behind us and we sank down on it together. There was no restraint at all, simply the knowledge that it was going to happen here and now at our own time and choosing.

No fumbling motions. Each move was deliberate, inviting, provoking the thing we both wanted so badly. Very slowly there was a release from the clothes that covered us, each in his own way doing what he wanted to do. I kissed her neck, uncovered her shoulders, and ran my mouth along them. When my hands cradled her breasts and caressed them they quivered at my touch, nuzzling my palms for more like a hungry animal.

133

Her stomach swelled gently against my fingers as I explored her, making her breath come in short, hard gasps. But even then there was no passiveness in her. She was as alive as I was, as demanding and as anxious. Her eyes told me of all the love she had for so long and the dreams she had had of its fulfillment.

The fiery contact of living flesh against living flesh was almost too much to stand and we had gone too far to refuse the demand any longer. She was mine and I was hers and we had to belong to each other.

But it didn't happen that way.

The doorbell rang like some damn screaming banshee and the suddenness of it wiped the *big now* right out of existence. I swore under my breath, then grinned at Velda, who swore back the same words and grinned too.

"When will it be, Mike?"

"Someday, kitten."

Before I could leave she grabbed my hand. "Make it happen."

"I will. Go get your clothes on."

The bell rang again, longer this time, and I heard Pat's voice calling out in the hall.

I yelled, "All right, damn it, hold on a minute."

He didn't take his finger off the bell until I had opened the door.

"I was on the phone," I explained. "Come on in."

There were four others with him, all men I had seen around the precinct. Two I knew from the old days and nodded to them. The others went through a handshake.

"Velda here?"

"Inside, why?"

"She was down asking questions around the party headquarters. They want an explanation. Charlie Force is pushing everybody around on this."

"So sit down and I'll explain."

Velda came out as they were pulling up chairs, met the officers and perched on the arm of the couch next to me. I laid it out for Pat to save him the time of digging himself, supplied him with Velda's notes and the names of the persons she spoke to, and wrapped it up with Art's little speech to me.

When Pat put his book away he said, "That's one

134

reason why I'm here. We're going to see what we can get on Howie Green. These officers have been working on it already and have come up with something that might get us started."

"Like what?"

"The real estate agency Howie Green operated went into the hands of his partner after his death. The guy's name was Quincy Malek. About a year later he contracted T.B. and died in six months. Now from a nephew we gather that Malek was damn near broke when he kicked off. He had sold out everything and his family picked over what was left. The original records left over from his partnership with Green went into storage somewhere, either private or commercial.

"Right now I have one bunch checking all the warehouses to see what they can dig up. The nephew does remember Malek asking that the records be kept so it's likely that they were. It wouldn't take up much room and a few hundred bucks would cover a storage bill on a small package for a long, long time.

"Now that's a supposition, the commercial angle. Malek and Green had a few other properties still in existence and we'll go through them too. Until everything is checked out you can't tell what we'll find. Meanwhile, we're taking another angle. We're checking all property transactions carried out by Green within a certain time of his death. If you're right something will show up. We'll check every damn one of them if we have to."

"You know how long it will take, Pat?"

"That's what I want to know. You got a better idea in that screwy mind of yours?"

"I don't know," I told him. "I'll have to think about it."

"Oh no, not you, boy. If you got anything you have it now. You just aren't the prolonged-thinking type. You got something going this minute and I want to know what it is."

"Stow it."

"Like that?"

"Like that. If it proves out I'll get it to you right away. The only reason I'm slamming it to you like this is because you're in deep enough as it is. Let me try my way. If there's trouble I'll take it alone."

"Mike . . . I don't like it. We have a killer running loose."

"Then let me be the target."

His eyes drifted to Velda beside me.

I said, "She'll stay safe. I went through that once before."

"Watch her," Pat said softly, and I knew he was never going to change about the way he felt for her.

"How many men you going to put through the files?"

"As many as I can spare."

"Suppose you get to it first?" I queried.

He smiled crookedly. "Well, with your official status I imagine I can pass on a tip to you. Just make sure it works both ways."

"Deal. How will we make contact?"

"Keep in touch with my office. If anything looks promising I'll leave word."

He got up to go and I reached for my coat. I picked the letter out and handed it to him. "It was in Sue's teddy bear. It puts a lock on Sim all the way. I don't advise showing it to the kid though."

Pat read it through once, shook his head, and put it in his inside coat pocket. "You're a card, man, a real card. What kind of luck have you got?"

"The best kind."

"Don't pull that kind of stunt on Grebb, buddy."

"You know me."

"Sure I know you."

I let them out and went back and stretched out on the couch. Velda made me some coffee and had one with me. I drank mine staring at the ceiling while I tried to visualize the picture from front to back. It was all there except the face. Blackie Conley's face. I knew I was going to see it soon. It was a feeling I had.

"Mike . . . where are we going?"

"You're thinking ahead of me, kiddo."

"Sometimes I have to."

"You're not going anyway."

"Don't cut me out, Mike." Her hand touched the side of my jaw, then traced a tingling line down my chin.

"Okay, doll."

"Want to tell me what you have in your mind?"

136

"A thought. The only thing that's wrong with the picture."

"Oh? What?"

"Why Blackie Conley would want to kill Sim."

"Mike . . ." She was looking past me, deep in thought. "Since it was Torrence who engineered that robbery and not Conley as you first thought, perhaps Conley suspected what was going to come off. Supposing he outguessed Torrence. In that case, he would have had the whole bundle to himself. He would have made his own getaway plans and broken out at the right time. Don't forget, Conley was older than Sonny and he was no patsy. There was no love between the pair either. In fact, Conley might even have guessed who the brain was behind the whole thing and had reasons for revenge."

"You might have something there, kitten."

"The first try was for Sue," she went on. "That really was an indirect blow at Sim. The next try was for them both."

"There's a possible flaw in your picture too, but I can supply an answer."

She waited. I said, "It's hard to picture a guy in his eighties going up that trellis. He'd have to hire it done . . . but that's why the hoods are in town."

"I don't know, Mike. Remember Bernarr Macfadden making his first parachute jump into the river when he was about the same age?"

"Uh-huh. It could be done."

"Then the answer is still to find Blackie Conley."

"That's right."

"How?"

"If we can restore another old man's memory we might get the answer."

"Sonny Motley?"

"Yup."

"Tonight?"

"Right now, sugar."

CHAPTER TEN

Finding Sonny Motley's apartment wasn't easy. Nobody in the gin mills knew where he lived; the cop on the beat around his store knew him but not his address. I checked the few newsstands that were open and they gave me a negative. It was at the last one that a hackie standing by heard me mention the name and said, "You mean that old con?"

"Yeah, the one who has the shoe shop."

"What's the matter?"

"Nothing. We need some information about a missing person and he might be able to help us."

"Ha, I'd like to see those old cons talk. They won't give nobody the right time."

"You know where he lives?"

"Sure. Took him home plenty of times. Hop in."

We climbed in the cab, went angling up to a shoddy section that bordered on the edge of Harlem, and the cabbie pointed out the place. "He's downstairs there on this side. Probably in bed by now."

"I'll get him up." I gave him a buck tip for his trouble and led the way down the sandstone steps to the iron gate at the bottom. I pushed the bell four or five times before a light came on inside.

A voice said, "Yeah, whatta ya want?"

"Sonny?"

"Who're you?"

"Mike Hammer."

"Oh, fer . . ." He came to the door, opened it, and reached for the grilled gate that held us out. He had a faded old robe wrapped around his body and a scowl on his face as black as night. Then he saw Velda and the sky lightened. "Hey . . . how about that."

"This is Velda, my secretary. Sonny Motley."

"Hello, Sonny."

"Well, don't just stand there. Come on in. Hot damn, I ain't had a broad in my joint since before I went to stir. Hot damn, this is great!" He slammed the gate, locked the door, and led the way down the hall. He

138

pushed his door open and said, "Don't mind the place, huh? So it's a crummy place and who comes here? I'm a crummy old man anyway. Sure feel good to have a broad in the joint. Want a drink?"

"I'll pass," I said.

"Not me." He grinned. "A sexy broad comes in like her and I'm gonna have me a drink."

"I thought you were all over the sex angle, Sonny."

"Maybe inside I am, but my eyes don't know it. No, sir. You sit down and let me get dressed. Be right back."

Sit down? We had a choice of box seats. Egg boxes or apple boxes. There was one old sofa that didn't look safe and a chair to match that had no cushion in it. The best bet was the arms of the chair so Velda took one side and I took the other.

A choice between living here or a nice comfortable prison would be easy to make. But like the man said, at least he was free. Sonny was back in a minute, hitching suspenders over bony shoulders, a bottle of cheap booze in his hand.

"You sure you don't want nothing?"

"No, thanks."

"No need to break out glasses then." He took a long pull from the bottle, ambled over to the couch, and sat down facing us. "Hot damn," he said, "those are the prettiest legs I ever saw."

Velda shifted uncomfortably, but I said, "That's what I keep telling her."

"You keep telling her, boy. They love to hear that kind of talk. Right, lady?"

She laughed at the impish look on his face. "I guess we can stand it."

"Damn right you can. Used to be a real killer with the ladies myself. All gone now though." He pulled at the bottle again. " 'Cept for looking. Guess a man never tires of looking." He set the bottle down on the floor between his feet and leaned back, his eyes glowing. "Now, what can I do for you?"

"I'm still asking questions, Sonny."

He waved his hands expansively. "Go ahead. If I can answer 'em it's all free."

"I can't get rid of the idea your old partner's still alive."

139

His shoulders jerked with a silent laugh. "Can't, eh? Well, you better, because that no-good is gone. Dead. I don't know where or how, but he's dead."

"Let's make like he isn't."

"I got lots of time."

"And I got news for you."

"How's that?"

"Sim Torrence is dead."

Briefly, his eyes widened. "True?"

"True."

Then he started to cackle again. "Good. Had it coming, the bugger. He put the screws on enough guys. I hope it wasn't easy."

"He was shot."

"Good. Bring the guy in and I'll fix his shoes free every time. I mean that. Free shine too."

"I thought you didn't care any more."

"Hell, I said I didn't hate him, not that I didn't care. So he's dead. I'm glad. Tomorrow I'll forget he was even alive. So what else is new?"

"Sim Torrence was the big brain who engineered your last job."

He was reaching for the bottle and stopped bent over. He looked up, not believing me. "Who says?"

"You'll read about it in the papers."

He straightened, the bottle entirely forgotten. "You mean . . ."

"Not only that, he engineered it right into a deliberate frame-up. That case made him the D.A. After that coup he was a landslide candidate."

"This is square, what you're telling me?"

"On the level, Sonny."

"The dirty son of a bitch. Sorry, lady."

"Here's an added note I want you to think about. If Blackie Conley got wise in time he could have worked the double-cross to his own advantage, taking the loot and dumping you guys."

Sonny sounded almost out of breath. "I'll be damned," he said. Some of the old fire was in his voice. "A real switcheroo. How do you like that? Sure, now I get what the score is. Blackie laid out the getaway route. Hell, he never followed through with the plan. He had something else schemed up and got away." Abruptly he dropped

140

his head and laughed at the floor. "Boy, he was smarter than I figured. How do you like that?" he repeated.

"Sonny . . ."

He looked up, a silly grin on his face. Egg. He couldn't get over it. I said, "Blackie rented the property you were supposed to hole up in from Howie Green."

"That's right."

"He must have bought another place at the same time for his own purpose using another name."

"Just like that bastard Green to fall in with him. He'd do anything for a buck. I'm glad Blackie knocked him off!"

"He did?"

"Sure he did. Before the heist. You think we wanted somebody knowing where we was headed?"

I looked at him, puzzled.

He caught the look and said, "Yeah, I know. There ain't no statute of limitations on murder. So they could still take me for being in it. Hell, you think I really care? Look around here. What do I have? Nothing. That's what. I already served life. What could they do that's worse? Maybe at the best I can live ten years, but what can I do with ten years? Live in a crummy rat hole? Beat on shoes all day? No friends? Man, it was better doin' time. You just don't know."

I waved him down. "Look, I don't care about Green. He asked for it, so he got it. I want Blackie Conley."

"How you gonna find him?"

"Did you know Green?"

"You kiddin'? Him and me grew up together on the same block. I took more raps for that punk when I was a kid . . . aw, forget it."

"Okay, now Green was a stickler for detail. He kept records somewhere. He passed on his business to his partner, Quincy Malek."

"I knew him too."

"Now Quincy kept the records. Wherever they are, they'll have a notation of the transactions carried out by the business. It will show the property locations and we can run them down one by one until we get the place Blackie bought from him."

"You think Blackie'll still be there?"

"He hasn't showed up any place else, has he?"

141

"That just ain't like Blackie." He rubbed his hands together and stared at them. "Maybe I didn't know Blackie so good after all. Now what?"

"Did you know Quincy Malek?"

"Sure. From kids yet. Him too. He was another punk."

"Where would he put something for safekeeping?"

"Quincy? Man, who knows?" He chuckled and leaned back against the cushions. "He had places all over. You know he operated a couple of houses without paying off? The boys closed him on that one."

"The records, Sonny. Right now we're checking up on all of Quincy's former properties and every commercial warehouse in the city, but if you remember anything about what he had you can cut the time right down."

"Mister, you're dragging me back thirty years."

"What did you have to think about all the time you were in prison, Sonny? Whatever it was belonged back there too because in prison there was nothing to think about."

"Broads," he grinned. "Until I was sixty all I thought about was broads. Not the used ones I had before, but ones that didn't even exist. Maybe after sixty I went back, but it took some time."

"Now you got something to think about."

Sonny sat there a long moment, then his mouth twisted into a sour grimace. "Tell me, mister. What would it get me? You it would get something. Me? Nothing. Trouble, that's all it would bring. Right now I ain't got nothin' but I ain't got trouble either. Nope. Don't think I can help you. I've had my belly full of trouble and now it's over. I don't want no more."

"There won't be trouble, Sonny."

"No? You think with all the papers down my throat I'd get any peace? You think I'd keep the lease on the shoe shop? It's bad enough I'm a con and a few people know it, but let everybody know it and I get booted right out of the neighborhood. No business, nothin'. Sorry, mister."

"There might be a reward in it."

"No dice. I'd have everybody in the racket chiseling it outa me. I'd wind up a drunk or dead. Somebody'd try to take me for the poke and I'd be out. Not me, Mister

142

Hammer. I'm too old to even worry about it."

Damn, he was tying me up tight and he was right. There had to be a way. I said, "If I wanted to I could put the heat on you for the Howie Green kill. The way things stand I wouldn't be a bit surprised if we got some quick and total cooperation from the police."

Sonny stared a second, then grunted. "What a guest *you* are. You sure want me to fall bad."

"Not that bad. If you want to push it I'd probably lay back. I'm just trying you, Sonny."

Once again his eyes caught Velda's legs. She had swung them out deliberately and the dress had pulled up over her knee. It was enough to make Sonny giggle again. "Oh, hell, why not? So maybe I can feed you something. What's it they call it? Public duty or some kind of crap like that."

"Quincy Malek, Sonny."

He sat back and squinted his eyes shut. "Now let's see. What would that punk do? He up and died but he never expected to, I bet. He was the kind who'd keep everything for himself if he could. Even if he left something to his family I bet they'd have to dig for it.

"Quincy owned property around town. Tenements, stuff like that. He'd buy cheap and hold. Got plenty in rentals and he seemed to know what was coming down and what was going up. Always had a hot iron in the fire."

"Would he keep any records there?"

"Nope, don't think so. Something might happen to 'em. My guess is he'd leave 'em with somebody."

"Who?"

"Something about old Quincy nobody knew. He kept a pair of sisters in an apartment building he owned. Tricky pair that. Real queer for anything different. I got the word once that he had a double deal with them. They owned the apartment with some papers signed so that he could take it back any time he wanted. He couldn't get screwed that way. Me, I'd look for those sisters. That building would be the only income they had and they couldn't dump it so they were stuck with it, but since it was a good deal all around, why not, eh?"

"Who were they, Sonny?"

"Now you got me, mister. I think if you poke around you'll find out who. I remember the deal, but not the dames. That any help?"

"It's a lead."

"Maybe I'll think of it later. You want me to call if I do?"

I picked a scrap of paper off the table, wrote down the office and home numbers, and gave them to him. "Keep calling these numbers until you get me or Velda here."

"Sure." He tucked the paper in his pants pocket. Then he got an idea. "Hey," he said, "if you find that crumb Blackie, you let me know. Hell, I'd even like a feel of that money. Just a feel. I think I'm entitled. It cost me thirty years."

"Okay, a feel," I said kiddingly.

Then Velda swung her leg out again and he grinned. "You know what I'd really like to feel, don't you?"

With a laugh Velda said, "You're a dirty old man."

"You bet, lady. But I'd sure like to see you with your clothes off just once."

"If you did you'd drop dead," I told him.

"What a way to go," he said.

Pat wasn't bothering to get any sleep either. I reached him at the office and gave him the dope Sonny passed on to me. He thought it had merit enough to start working on and was going to put two men on it right away. Nothing else had paid off yet, although they had come up with a few former properties Malek had owned. They had made a search of the premises, but nothing showed. A team of experts were on a twenty-four-hour detail in the records section digging up old titles, checking possibles, and having no luck at all so far.

Offhand I asked for Quincy's old address and Pat gave me the location of his home and the building the real estate agency was housed in. He had checked them both personally and they were clean.

I hung up the phone and asked Velda if she wanted something to eat. The Automat was right down the street so she settled for a cup of coffee and a sandwich. We waited for the light, cut over, and ducked inside.

Right at the front table Jersey Toby was having coffee

and when he saw me he simply got up and left with his coffee practically untouched.

We fed nickels into the slots, got what we wanted, and picked a table.

Outside the damn rain had started again.

Velda said, "What's on your mind?"

"How can you tell?"

"Your poker face slipped. You're trying to think of something."

I slammed the coffeecup down. "One lousy thing. I can feel it. One simple goddamn thing I can't put my finger on and it's right there in front of me. I keep forgetting things."

"It'll come back."

"Now is when I need it."

"Will talking about it help?"

"No."

"You're close, aren't you?"

"We're sitting right on top of it, baby. We're riding three million bucks into the ground and have a killer right in front of us someplace. The damn guy is laughing all the way too."

"Suppose the money isn't there?"

"Honey . . . you don't just *lose* that kind of capital. You don't misplace it. You put it someplace for a purpose. Somebody is ready to move in this town and that money is going to buy that person a big piece of action. If that one is as smart as all this, the action is going to be rough and expensive."

"Why don't you call Pat again? They might have something."

"I don't want to bug him to death."

"He won't mind."

We pushed away from the table and found a phone booth. Pat was still at his desk and it was three A.M. He hadn't found anything yet. He did have one piece of news for me and I asked what it was.

"We picked up one of the out-of-town boys who came in from Detroit. He was getting ready to mainline one when he got grabbed and lost his fix. He sweated plenty before he talked; now he's flipping because he's in trouble. The people who sent him here won't have anything to do with a junkie and if they know he's on H he's dead. Now he's yelling for protection."

"Something hot?"

"We know the prime factor behind the move into town. Somebody has spent a lot of time collecting choice items about key men in the Syndicate operation. He's holding it over their heads and won't let go. The payoff is for them to send in the best enforcers who are to be the nucleus of something new and for this they're paying and keeping still about it. None of them wants to be caught in a bind by the Syndicate itself so they go with the demand."

"Funny he'd know that angle."

"Not so funny. Their security isn't that good. Word travels fast in those circles. I bet we'll get the same story if we can put enough pressure on any of the others."

"You said they were clean."

"Maybe we can dirty them up a little. In the interest of justice, that is."

"Sometimes it's the only way. But tell me this, Pat . . . who could pull a play like that? You'd need to know the in of the whole operation. That takes some big smarts. You'd have to pinpoint your sucker and concentrate on him. This isn't a keyhole game."

"It's been done."

"Blackie Conley could have done it," I suggested. "He could have used a bite of the loot for expenses and he would have had the time and the know-how."

"That's what I think too."

"Anything on Malek's women?"

"Hold it a minute." I heard him put the phone down, speak to somebody, then he picked it up again. "Got a note here from a retired officer who was contacted. He remembers the girls Malek used to run with but can't recall the building. His second wife put in a complaint to have it raided for being a disorderly house at one time and he was on the call. Turned out to be a nuisance complaint and nothing more. He can't place the building any more though."

"Hell," I said.

"We'll keep trying. Where will you be?"

"Home. I've had it."

"See you tomorrow," Pat said.

I hung up and looked at Velda. "Malek," I said. "Nobody can find where he spent his time."

"Why don't you try the yellow pages?" Velda kidded.

I paused and nodded. "You just might be right at that, kid."

"It was a joke, Mike."

I shook my head. "Pat just told me he had a second wife. That meant he had a first. Let's look it up."

There were sixteen Maleks in the directory and I got sixteen dimes to make the calls. Thirteen of them told me everything from drop dead to come on up for a party, but it was the squeaky old voice of the fourteenth that said yes, she was Mrs. Malek who used to be married to Quincy Malek. No, she never used the Quincy or the initial because she never cared for the name. She didn't think it was the proper time to call, but yes, if it was as important as I said it was, I could come right over.

"We hit something, baby," I said.

"Pat?"

"Not yet. Let's check this one out ourselves first."

The cab let us out on the corner of Eighth and Forty-ninth. Somewhere along the line over one of the store fronts was the home of Mrs. Quincy Malek the first. Velda spotted the number over the darkened hallway and we went in, found the right button, and pushed it. Seconds later a buzzer clicked and I opened the door.

It was only one flight up. The stairs creaked and the place reeked of fish, but the end could be up there.

She was waiting at the top of the landing, a garishly rouged old lady in a feathered wrapper that smelled of the twenties and looked it. Her hair was twisted into cloth curlers with a scarf hurriedly thrown over it and she had that querulous look of all little old ladies suddenly yanked out of bed at a strange hour.

She forced a smile, asked us in after we introduced ourselves, and had us sit at the kitchen table while she made tea. Neither Velda nor I wanted it, but if she were going to put up with us we'd have to go along with her.

Only when the tea was served properly did she ask us what we wanted.

I said, "Mrs. Malek . . . it's about your husband."

"Oh, he died a long time ago."

147

"I know. We're looking for something he left behind."

"He left very little, very little. What he left me ran out years ago. I'm on my pension now."

"We're looking for some records he might have kept."

"My goodness, isn't that funny?"

"What is?"

"That you should want them too."

"Who else wanted them, Mrs. Malek?"

She poured another cup of tea for me and put the pot down daintily. "Dear me, I don't know. I had a call . . . oh, some months ago. They wanted to know if Quincy left any of his business records with me. Seems that they needed something to clear up a title."

"Did he, Mrs. Malek?"

"Certainly, sir. I was the only one he could ever trust. He left a large box with me years ago and I kept it for him as I said I would in case it was ever needed."

"This party who called . . ."

"I told him what I'm telling you."

"Him?"

"Well . . . I really couldn't say. It was neither a man's nor a woman's voice. They offered me one hundred dollars if they could inspect the box and another hundred if I were instrumental in proving their claim."

"You take it?"

Her pale blue eyes studied me intently. "Mr. Hammer, I am no longer a woman able to fend for herself. At my age two hundred dollars could be quite an asset. And since those records had been sitting there for years untouched, I saw no reason why I shouldn't let them have them."

It was like having a tub of ice water dumped over you. Velda sat there, the knuckles of her hand white around the teacup.

"Who did you give it to, Mrs. Malek?"

"A delivery boy. He left me an envelope with one hundred dollars in it."

"You know the boy?"

"Oh dear no. He was just . . . a boy. Spanish, I think. His English was very bad."

"Damn," I said.

"Another cup of tea, Mr. Hammer?"

"No, thanks." Another cup of tea would just make

148

me sick. I looked at Velda and shook my head.

"The box was returned, of course," she said suddenly.

"What!"

"With another hundred dollars. Another boy brought it to me."

"Look, Mrs. Malek . . . if we can take a look at that box and find what we're looking for, I'll make a cash grant of five hundred bucks. How does that sound to you?"

"Lovely. More tea?"

I took another cup of tea. This one didn't make me sick. But she almost did. She sat there until I finished the cup, then excused herself and disappeared a few minutes. When she came back she was carrying a large cardboard carton with the top folded down and wrapped in coarse twine.

"Here you are, Mr. Hammer."

Velda and I opened the carton carefully, flipped open the top, and looked down at the stacked sheafs of notations that filled the entire thing. Each one was an independent sales record that listed prices, names, and descriptions and there were hundreds of them. I checked the dates and they were spread through the months I wanted.

"Are you satisfied, sir?"

I reached for my wallet and took out five bills. There were three singles left. I laid them on the table but she didn't touch them.

She said, "One of those pieces of paper is missing, I must tell you."

All of a sudden I had that sick feeling again. I looked at the five hundred bucks lying on the table and so did Mrs. Malek.

"How do you know?" I asked her.

"Because I counted them. Gracious, when Quincy trusted me with them I wanted to be sure they were always there. Twice a year I used to go through them to make sure the tally was identical with the original one. Then when I got them back I counted them again and one was missing." She looked at me and nodded firmly. "I'm positive. I counted twice."

"That was the one we wanted, Mrs. Malek."

"I may still be of help." She was smiling at some private secret. "Some years back I was sick. Quite sick. I was

149

here in bed for some months and for lack of something to do I decided to make my own record of Quincy's papers. I listed each and every piece much as he did."

She reached into the folds of her wrapper and brought out a thick, cheap note pad and laid it down on the table. "You'll have to go through them all one by one and find the piece that's missing, but it's here, Mr. Hammer."

I picked up the pad, hefted it, and stuck it in my pocket. "One question, Mrs. Malek. Why are you going so far with us?"

"Because I don't like to be stolen from. That other party deliberately stole something of value from me. That person was dishonest. Therefore I assume you are honest. Am I wrong?"

"You aren't wrong, Mrs. Malek. You may get more out of this than you think."

"This is sufficient for my needs, sir."

I picked up the box and put on my hat. "You'll get them all back this time. The police may want to hold them for a while, but eventually they'll be returned."

"I'm sure they will. And I thank you, sir."

I grinned at her. "I could kiss you."

"That would be a pleasure." She glanced at Velda. "Do you mind?"

"Be my guest," Velda said.

So I kissed her.

Damn if the blush didn't make the rouge spots fade right out.

The last three bucks bought a cab ride back to the apartment and two hamburgers apiece. We dumped the contents of the box on the floor, spread them out into piles, opened the notebook, and started to go through them.

At dawn I called Pat without telling him what I had. So far he had nothing. Then we went back to the scoreboard. It could have taken a few days but we got lucky. At three in the afternoon Velda instituted a quick system of cross-checking and we found the missing item.

It was a deed made out to one Carl Sullivan for a piece of property in Ulster County, New York, and the location was accurately described. Beneath it, apparently copied from the original notation, were the initials, B.C. *Blackie Conley!*

150

I had to borrow fifty bucks from George over at the Blue Ribbon to get on my way, but he came up with the dough and no questions. Down the street I rented a Ford and Velda got in it for the drive upstate. Instead of taking the Thruway I got on old Route 17 and stopped at Central Valley to see a real estate dealer I knew. It wasn't easy to keep the glad-handing and old-times talk to a minimum, but we managed. I gave him my property location and he pulled down a wall map and started locating it on the grid.

He found it quickly enough. Then he looked at me strangely and said, "You own this?"

"No, but I'm interested in it."

"Well, if you're thinking of buying it, forget it. This is in the area they located those gas wells on and several big companies have been going nuts trying to find the owner. It's practically jungle up there and they want to take exploration teams in and can't do it without permission. The taxes have been paid in advance so there's no squawk from the state and nobody can move an inch until the owner shows up."

"Tough."

His face got a little bit hungry. "Mike . . . do you know the owner?"

"I know him."

"Think we can swing a deal?"

"I doubt it."

His face fell at the thought of the money he was losing. "Well, if he wants to sell, put in a word for me, okay?"

"I'll mention it to him."

That seemed to satisfy him. We shook hands back at the car and took off. An hour and ten minutes later we were at the turnoff that led to the property. The first road was a shale and dirt one that we took for a mile, looking for a stream. We found that too, and the barely visible indentation that showed where another road had been a long time back.

I drove down the road and backed the Ford into

the bushes, hiding it from casual observation, then came back to Velda and looked at the jungle we were going into.

The trees were thick and high, pines intermingled with oaks and maples, almost hopelessly tangled at their bases with heavy brush and thorny creepers. Towering overhead was the uneven roll of the mountain range.

It was getting late and we wouldn't have too much sun left.

"It's someplace in there," I said. "I don't know how he did it, but it was done. He's in there."

Animals had made their way in ahead of us. The trail was barely visible and some of the brush was fuzzed with the hair of deer, the earth, where it was soft in spots, showing the print of their hoofs. We made it crawling sometimes, fighting the undergrowth constantly. But little by little we got inside.

The ground slope ranged upward, leveled off, then slanted down again. We saw the remains of a shack and headed toward it, but that was all it was, a vermin-infested building that had long ago fallen into ruin. At one side there was a carton of rusted tins that had spilled over and rotted out, and another wooden crate of cooking utensils, still nested inside each other. The remains of a mattress had been scattered over the floor making permanent nests for thousands of mice.

It didn't make sense.

We started down the slope and burst through the brush into a clearing that was shaped like a bowl. Nature had somehow started something growing there, a peculiar soft grass that refused to allow anything else to intrude on its domain.

Velda said, "Mike . . ."

I stopped and looked back.

"I'm tired, Mike. Can't we rest a minute?"

"Sure, honey. This is a good place."

She sank to the ground with a long sigh and stretched out languidly looking at the sky. The clouds were tinged with a deep red and the shadows were beginning to creep down the mountainside. "This is lovely, Mike."

"Not much like the city, is it?"

She laughed, said, "No," and lifted her legs to strip off the ruins of her nylons. She stopped with one leg

152

pointed toward the mountain. "You do it."

What a broad.

I held her foot against my stomach, unhooked the snaps that held the stockings, and peeled one down, then the other. She said, "Ummm," and patted the ground beside her. I crossed my legs and sat down, but she grabbed for me, tipped me over toward her, and held my face in her hands. "It's going to be dark soon, Mike. We can't go back through that again. Not until morning." Her smile was impish.

"Any time, any place. You're crazy."

"I want you, Mike. Now."

"It's going to get cold."

"Then we'll suffer."

I kissed her then, her mouth slippery against mine.

"It's awfully warm now," she murmured. She raised her legs and the dress slid down her thighs.

"Stop that."

Her hand took mine and held it against the roundness of one thigh, keeping it there until she could take hers away and knew mine would stay. Ever so slowly my hand began a movement of its own, sensing the way to love, unable to stop the motion.

With an age-old feminine motion she made it easier for me, her entire being trying to bring me into its vortex and I tried to fill the void. There was something I was fighting against, but it wasn't a fight I knew I could win. There was a bulk between us and Velda's hand reached inside my coat and pulled out the .45 and laid it on the ground in back of her.

The sun was low now, the rays angling into the trees. One of them picked up a strange color in the brush at the foot of the hill, an odd color that never should have been there. I stared at it, trying to make out what it was.

Then I knew.

The fingers of my hand squeezed involuntarily and Velda let out a little cry, the pain of it shocking her. I said, "Stay here," and snapped to my feet.

"Mike . . ."

I didn't take the time to answer her. I ran down the hill toward the color and with each step it took shape and form until it was what I knew it had to be.

153

A thirty-year-old taxi cab. A yellow and black taxi that had been stolen off the streets back in the thirties.

The tires were rotted shreds now, but the rest of it was intact. Only a few spots of rust showed through the heavy layers of paint that the cab had been coated with to protect it against the destruction of the wind-driven grit in the city.

I looked it over carefully and almost wanted to say that they sure didn't make them like this any more. The windows were still rolled shut hard against their rubber cushions so that the stuff fused them right into the body of the car with age. The car had been new when it was stolen, and they made that model to last for years. It was an airtight vault now, a bright yellow, wheeled mausoleum for two people.

At least they had been two people.

Now they were two mummies. The one in the front was slumped across the wheel, hat perched jauntily on a skeletal head covered with drawn, leathery flesh. There wasn't much to the back of the head. That had been blown away.

The guy who did it was the other mummy in the back seat. He leaned against the other side of the car, his mouth gaping open so that every tooth showed, his clothes hanging from withered limbs. Where his eyes were I could see two little dried bits of things that still had the appearance of watching me.

He still held the rifle across his lap aimed at the door in front of me, fingers clutched around its stock and his right forefinger still on the trigger. There was a black stain of blood on the shirt that could still give it a startlingly white background.

Between his feet were three canvas sacks.

A million dollars in each.

I had finally found Blackie Conley.

She came up on bare feet and I didn't hear her until her breath hissed with the horror of what she saw. She pressed the back of her hand against her mouth to stop the scream that started to come, her eyes wide open for long moments.

"Mike . . . who . . . ?"

"Our killer, Velda. The Target. The one we were after. That's Blackie Conley in the back seat there. He

154

almost made it. How close can a guy come?"

"Pretty close, Mr. Hammer. Some of us come all the way."

I didn't hear him either! He had come up the side of the hill on sneakered feet and stood there with a gun on us and I felt like the biggest fool in the world! My .45 was back there in the love nest and now we were about to be as dead as the others. It was like being right back at the beginning again.

I said, "Hello, Sonny."

The Snake. The real snake, as deadly as they come. The only one that had real fangs and knew how to use them. His face had lost the tired look and his eyes were bright with the desirous things he saw in his future. There was nothing stooped about him now, nothing of the old man there. Old, yes, but he wasn't the type who grew old easily. It had all been a pose, a cute game, and he was the winner.

"You scared me, Mr. Hammer. When you got as far as Malek you really scared me. I was taking my time about coming here because I wasn't ready yet and then I knew it was time to move. You damn near ruined everything." What I used to call a cackle was a pose too. He did have a laugh. He thought it was funny.

Velda reached for my arm and I knew she was scared. It was too much too fast all over again and she could only take so much.

"Smart," he said to me. "You're a clever bastard. If all I had was the cops to worry about it would have been no trouble, but I had to draw you." His mouth pulled into a semblance of a grin. "Those nice talks we had. You kept me right up to date. Tell me, did you think I had a nice face?"

"I thought you had more sense, Sonny."

He dropped the grin then. "Get off it, guy. More sense? For what? You think I was going to spend all my life in the cooler without getting some satisfaction? Mister, that's where you made your mistake. You should have gone a little further into my case history. I always was a mean one because it paid off. If I had to play pretty-face to make it pay off I could do that too."

"You won't make it, Sonny."

"No? Well, just lose that idea. For thirty years I

155

worked this one out. I had all the time in the world to do it too. With the contacts I had in the can I got enough on the big boys to make them jump my way when I was ready. I put together a mob and now I'll have to move to get it rolling. You think I won't live big for what little time I have left? Well, you're making a mistake when you think that. A lot of planning went into this dodge, kid."

"You still hate, don't you?"

Sonny Motley nodded slowly, a smile of pure pleasure forming. "You're goddamn right. I hated that bastard Torrence and tried to get at him through his kid. Mistake there . . . I thought he loved the kid. I would've been doin' him a favor to rub her out, right?"

"He was trying for her too."

"I got the picture fast enough. When I knocked him off in his house I thought I'd get the kid just for the fun of it. She fooled me. Where was she, mister?"

I shrugged.

"Hell, it don't matter none now." He lifted the gun so I could see down the barrel. "I thought sure you'd get on to me sooner. I pulled a boner, you know that, don't you?"

I knew it now, all right. When Marv Kania tried to nail me with the cab it was because Sonny had called him from the back room when he faked getting me old clippings of his crime and told him where I was going. When Marv almost got me in my apartment it was because Sonny told him my new address and that I'd be there. I made it easy because I told Sonny both times.

I said, "Marv Kania was holed up in your place, wasn't he?"

"That's right, dying every minute, and all he wanted was to get that last crack at you. It was the one thing that kept him alive."

"It was the thing that killed him too, Sonny."

"Nobody'll miss him but me. The kid had guts. He knew nobody could help him, but he stuck the job out."

"You got the guts too, Sonny?"

"I got the guts, Hammer." He laughed again. "You gave old Blackie credit for having my guts though. That was pretty funny. You were so sure it was him. Never

156

me. Blackie the slob. You know, I figured out that cross when I was in stir. It came through to me and when I put the pieces together bit by bit I knew what I was going to do. I even figured out how Blackie got wise at the last minute and what he'd do to plan a getaway. He wasn't such a hard guy to second-guess. After all, I had thirty years to do it in. Now it's the big loot I waited all that time to spend."

"You won't do it, Sonny."

"How you figure to stop me? You got no gun and you're under one. I can pump a fast one into you both and nobody will hear a sound. Blackie picked this place pretty well. You're gonna die, you know. I can't let you two run around."

Velda's fingers bit into my arm harder. "See the money in the car, Hammer? It still there? It wasn't in the shack so it's gotta be there or around here somewhere."

"Look for yourself."

"Step back."

We moved slowly, two steps, then stood there while Sonny grinned and looked into the window of the cab.

It was hard to tell what was happening to his face. For one second I thought I'd have a chance to jump him but he caught himself in time and swung the gun back on us. His eyes were dancing with the joy of the moment and the laugh in his throat was real.

Sonny Motley was doing what he had wanted to do for so long, meeting Blackie Conley face to face.

"Look at him. It's him back there! Look at that dirty double-crosser sitting there just like I shot him. Goddamn, I didn't miss with that shot. I killed the son of a bitch thirty years ago! See that, Hammer . . . see the guy I killed thirty years ago. Damn, if that isn't a pretty sight."

He paused, sucking in his breath, his chest heaving. "Just like he was, still got that rifle he loved. See where I got him, Hammer . . . right in the chest. Right through the open window before he could get his second shot off.

"Hello, Blackie, you dirty bastard!" he shrieked. "How'd you like that shot? How'd it feel to die, Blackie? This is worth waiting all the thirty years for!"

Sonny turned and grimaced at me, his eyes burning. "Always figured to make it, Blackie did. Had the driver pull him into his hidey hole and shot him in the head. But he never lived through my shot. No chance of that. Man, this is my *big* day . . . the biggest damn day in my life! Now I got everything!"

He drew himself erect at the thought, a funny expression changing his face. He said, "Only one thing I ain't got any more," and this time he was looking at Velda.

"Take those clothes off, lady."

Her fingers that were so tight on my arm seemed to relax and I knew she was thinking the same thing as I was. It could be a diversion. If she could step aside and do it so we were split up I might get the chance to jump him.

I didn't watch her. I couldn't. I had to watch him. But I could tell from his eyes just what she was doing. I knew when she took the skirt off, then the bra. I watched his eyes follow her hands as she slid the skirt down over her ankles and I knew by the quick intake of his breath and the sudden brightness of his eyes when she had stepped out of the last thing she wore.

She made the slightest motion to one side then, but he was with it. He said, "Just stay there, lady. Stay there close where I can get to you both."

Not much time was left now. The fire in his eyes was still burning, but it wouldn't last.

"Real nice, lady," he said. "I like brunettes. Always have. Now you can die like that, right together."

No time at all now.

"Too bad you didn't get the money, Sonny."

He shook his head at me, surprised that I'd make such a bad attempt. "It's right on the floor there."

"You'd better be sure, Sonny. We got here ahead of you."

If he had trouble opening the door I might be able to make the move. All he had to do was falter once and if I could get past the first shot I could take him even if he caught me with it. Velda would hit the ground the second he pulled the trigger and together we'd have him.

"No good, Hammer. It's right there and Old Blackie is still guarding it with his rifle. You saw it."

"You didn't."

"Okay, so you get one last look." He reached for the door handle and gave it a tentative tug. It didn't budge. He laughed again, knowing what I was waiting for but not playing it my way at all. The gun never wavered and I knew I'd never get the chance. From where he stood he could kill us both with ease and we all knew it.

The next time he gave the door a sharp jerk and it swung open, the hinges groaning as the rust ground into them. He was watching us with the damndest grin I ever saw and never bothered to see what was happening in the cab. The pull on the door was enough to rock the car and ever so steadily the corpse of Blackie Conley seemed to come to life, sitting up in the seat momentarily. I could see the eyes and the mouth open in a soundless scream with the teeth bared in a grimace of wild hatred.

Sonny knew something was happening and barely turned his head to look . . . just enough to see the man he had killed collapse into dust fragments, and as it did the bony finger touched the trigger that had been filed to react to the smallest of pressures and the rifle squirted a blossom of roaring flame that took Sonny Motley square in the chest and dropped him lifeless four feet away.

While the echo still rumbled across the mountainside, the leather-covered skull of Blackie Conley bounced out of the cab and rolled to a stop face to face with Sonny and lay there grinning at him idiotically.

You can only sustain emotion so long. You can only stay scared so long. It stops and suddenly it's like nothing happened at all. You don't shake, you don't break up. You're just glad it's over. You're a little surprised that your hands aren't trembling and wonder why it is you feel almost perfectly normal.

Velda said quietly, "It's finished now, isn't it?"

Her clothes were in a heap beside her and in the dying rays of the sun she looked like a statuesque wood nymph, a lovely naked wood nymph with beautiful black hair as dark as a raven against a sheen of molded flesh that rose and dipped in curves that were unbelievable.

Up there on the hill the grass was soft where we had lain in the nest. It smelled flowery and green and the night was going to be a warm night. I looked at her, then toward the spot on the hill. Tomorrow it would be something else, but this was now.

I said, "You ready?"

She smiled at me, savoring what was to come. "I'm ready."

I took her hand, stepped over the bodies, new and old, on the ground, and we started up the slope.

"Then let's go," I said.